J.J., Navajo Princess

Renée Kent

3

J.J., Navajo Princess

Renée Kent

New Hope® Publishers

Birmingham, Alabama

New Hope® Publishers
P.O. Box 12065
Birmingham, AL 35202-2065
www.newhopepubl.com

Library of Congress Cataloging-in-Publication Data

Kent, Renee Holmes, 1955-
  JJ , Navajo princess / Renee Holmes Kent.
    p. cm. -- (Adventures in Misty Falls ; bk. 3)
Summary: Eager to know more about her Navajo family and to understand
why she and her mother left them, J.J. gratefully accepts the help of
friends.
  ISBN 1-56309-763-x
  [1. Christian life--Fiction.
  2. Identity--Fiction.
  3. Navajo Indians--Fiction.
  4. Indians of North America--Southwest,
New--Fiction.] I. Title. PZ7.K419 Jj 2000
  [Fic]--dc21 99-050712

Cover design by Todd Cotton
Cover illustration by Matt Archambault

ISBN: 1-56309-763-X
N007105 • 0400 • 7.5M1

Misty Falls, Georgia

J.J., Navajo Princess

1

Ba-la-bump. Ba-la-bump. Gracie's smooth canter caused Jennifer Joy Graystone's long dark braid to beat a steady drum cadence against her relaxed shoulders. Happiness bubbled within her and spilled over into her clear, indigo eyes. Whenever she was on horseback, she felt as if she sparkled, like Misty Falls—the nearby waterfall tumbling over river rocks.

Horseback riding with her best friend Cassie Holbrook was just about the most fun in the whole world, especially at the Holbrook family's farm on the outskirts of Misty Falls. The huge farm was a perfect place to ride for hours on end. J.J. and Cassie never got bored exploring the woods of Possum Creek at the edge of the farm.

In the practice arena just before sunset, J.J. easily rode her sleek chestnut mare, Gracie, bareback style. Cassie watched intently from atop the fence railing. Chester, Cassie's black and white spotted pony, snorted lazily. He paid no attention to

Gracie and J.J. as he nibbled at tufts of tender grasses that had grown greener and sweeter around the fence posts.

The girls had just finished their daily chores at the Holbrook farm. Though it was hard work, J.J. didn't mind. After all, Cassie's family was allowing her to board her horse, Gracie, there for free, in exchange for doing the chores that Mr. Holbrook assigned.

"Oh Cassie," J.J. bubbled, "I love your family so much. Thanks again for letting me board Gracie here. I can tell she's so happy. See the way she prances and perks up her ears?"

"Yes," agreed Cassie. "Gracie loves being on the farm. Besides, she keeps silly old Chester out of trouble!" Cassie reached over to stroke her pony's shaggy mane.

"What a close call," J.J. said, remembering last week. She had almost lost Gracie forever. "Do you realize that my mom almost had to *sell* Gracie? If your parents hadn't offered to let me work for Gracie's board, we wouldn't be able to afford to keep her!"

Cassie smiled. "I guess Mom is right. She often quotes that Bible verse that says, 'Everything works out for the best for those who love the Lord.' Anyway, it goes something like that."

"I don't know," said J.J. "Things never seem to work out quite the way you expect them to."

"Yeah, no kidding! Remember the fair? That didn't

J.J., Navajo Princess

turn out anything like I expected," said Cassie. She could laugh now that her runaway pony adventure and Snickerdoodle disaster were both over.

"Still, you're right. God did seem to make everything turn out fine, didn't He!" J.J. exclaimed as she rode past Cassie and Chester again. "If you hadn't baked Snickerdoodles for the fair, you wouldn't have been invited by the fair judge to bake cookies for the blood drive."

"And if we hadn't baked cookies for the blood drive," said Cassie, "we wouldn't have met Nurse Trixie and Robyn and the rest of our new friends at New Hope Center."

"Oh wow," exclaimed J.J. "You're right! God did work out everything for the best. Better than best!"

For a while the girls didn't speak. J.J. focused on her riding skills, as Cassie watched from her perch on the fence railing. J.J. became so intent on what she was doing that she almost forgot that Cassie was watching. Her imagination began to take her far, far away from Misty Falls...almost two thousand miles west to Arizona.

For the next few moments, she and Gracie were racing across the hot desert mesa under a perfectly crisp, blue sky. They were racing to Grandmother's old sun-baked hogan for supper. J.J. smiled to herself, thinking how surprised Grandmother Teresa (*teh-ray-sah*) would be, if she burst into the doorway of the one-room hogan just in time for a meal of fry bread and honey.

"Excuse me, but how do you do that?" Cassie's question startled J.J., and her mind returned to Misty Falls. When she saw Cassie's expression, J.J. burst into giggles. The most comical look of amazement was plastered on her friend's fair face, which was freckled from the late summer sun.

J.J. thought she already knew what Cassie wanted to know, but she asked, "How do I do what?"

As Gracie continued pacing about the practice ring, Cassie sighed impatiently as only Cassie could. "How do you ride a horse without a saddle? I mean, there's no saddle horn for you to hold onto or stirrups for your feet. What keeps you from falling to the ground?"

J.J. grinned. She loved to keep poor Cass in suspense. "Of course there is something to hold onto. I hold onto the horse, of course!" she said with amusement.

"But how?" wondered Cassie aloud. With a shrug, she explained why she wanted to know. "Once I tried to ride Chester bareback and fell off when he took the first step! But you aren't even using the reins. You're not holding on at all."

"Oh, yes I am," said J.J. mysteriously. Keeping Cassie guessing was just plain fun. "You just can't see *how* I'm holding on."

Finally, Cassie put her hands on her hips. "So? Are

J.J., Navajo Princess

you going to tell me how you are staying on top of Gracie or not?"

J.J. laughed aloud. "Okay, I will tell you. My legs are doing all the work. See? I'm squeezing Gracie's middle with my thighs. I can hold on just fine that way. I can also steer her with my legs. Who needs a bridle and saddle?"

Cassie's hazel eyes grew wider. "I do!" she declared. "J.J., you're a natural-born rider."

"I know," said J.J. "It's sort of in my blood. My ancestors used to ride like this out west. Mom told me so."

This time, Cassie's sigh was sort of dreamy, as she studied Gracie and J.J.'s fluid moves around the practice ring. "Wow," she said. "I don't think I could do that. What am I saying? I *know* I couldn't do that!"

"Sure you could," said J.J. "It takes some practice and a safe, trustworthy horse. But there's not a more fun way to ride!"

Without a doubt, riding bareback was J.J.'s favorite way to travel. It was an awesome experience to feel all of Gracie's muscles working beneath her.

After years of riding Gracie, J.J. had come to know her horse like a family member. She realized that she had a special relationship with her mare that could only come with lots of time spent together. J.J. and Gracie trusted each other. J.J. was patient and loving with Gracie, and Gracie was patient and loving with J.J.

That's why J.J. trusted Gracie's "good horse heart."

5

Gracie always took care of her, whenever she was aboard that strong, sleek back. Gracie even seemed to watch for exposed tree roots, potholes, or anything else that might upset J.J.'s balance. In her opinion, she was the most wonderful horse ever.

"Watch this, Cass," she said, continuing to retrace the hoofprints of the riding ring. First, she closed her eyes. Then she flung out her arms freely in the air. J.J. heard Cassie gasp with alarm. But J.J. felt as calm as a glassy sea.

As Gracie made her even strides, J.J. continued to hold out her arms. In a spirit of victory, she proclaimed, "See? I'm *Nascha,* a Navajo princess. *Nascha* is Grandmother Teresa's name for me."

Cassie gasped again. J.J. joggled up and down upon Gracie's back with each step.

"Princess or no princess! Jennifer Joy Graystone, you stop that!" Cassie demanded. "You're scaring me to pieces!" But J.J. only laughed. Making Cassie "squirm" was such fun!

J.J. loved this method of "feeling" her way around the ring. When she closed her eyes and let go, she could become one with her horse. It was a feeling that she knew Cassie couldn't share—at least not yet.

All J.J. had to do was cluck and gently squeeze Gracie's sides with her legs. Gracie would readily obey. The mare always seemed to know just what J.J. wanted her to do, which was why J.J. trusted her horse as much as she trusted her friendship with Cassie.

"J.J., I just don't want you to fall and get hurt," said Cassie, who was a beginner at riding. She was even more cautious than usual, after her frightening ride on Chester at the fair.

Without warning, J.J. threw her head back and let out a "whoop." Startled, Cassie nearly fell off the fence railing. "Hey, what's the big idea?" she scolded.

"Sorry, Cass!" J.J. said, "Don't be alarmed. I just feel so, so...free!"

That free feeling came anytime she was riding Gracie. She always loved pretending that she was back on the Navajo Reservation with Grandmother Teresa. Even though J.J. only remembered a few Navajo words, and Grandmother only knew a few English words, they understood each other's hearts very well.

Most of the time, J.J. felt glad to live in Misty Falls with her mom and her cat, Frisco. After all, she had the best friends ever in Georgia—especially Cassie, Iggy Potts, and more recently, her new friends Robyn Morgan and Hunter Harris. Still, she missed Grandmother.

"Are you thinking about Grandmother Teresa again?" Cassie asked. Cassie always seemed to know what J.J. was thinking, except about horse matters. "I wish I could meet her."

J.J. smiled. "You know me very well," she said.

"When I was a little girl and lived on the Navajo

Reservation, I sometimes stayed with my grandmother in the old hogan. When Mom and I moved to Misty Falls, I cried for Grandmother every night. Even now, I still sometimes dream I am with her in the canyon, tending sheep or selling turquoise jewelry to the tourists."

Suddenly J.J. realized Gracie had slowed to a walk. "Come up, girl," she instructed.

In reply, Gracie shook her head in a "yes" motion, snorted, and began to trot briskly around the ring. J.J.'s laughter floated once again through the cool, evening air.

"Wow, you and Gracie are amazing!" Cassie exclaimed. "I wish Chester and I could look that graceful. Fat chance!"

"Oh Cassie, you've only been riding for a year or so. Gracie and I have been together since I was six. Remember, I got her right after I moved to Misty Falls."

Cassie hopped off the fence railing and dusted off her jeans. She rubbed the nose of her lovable, pot-bellied pony. Chester nickered softly and nuzzled Cassie's pockets for sugar cubes.

"Hey, boy! You're always thinking about food," she said with amusement. "You've been a grazing machine all day. Isn't your stomach ever full?"

Cassie firmly grasped a handful of Chester's mane and the saddle horn. She mounted her pony and slid her feet snugly into the stirrups. "See, J.J.? This is the safe way to ride, you know, with a saddle and bridle?"

J.J. couldn't help giggling. That was what J.J. loved most about Cassie. They were exact opposites, but they got along perfectly. "Oh come on, let go and see how much fun it is!" she urged.

"No, thank you!" Cassie shook her head until her light auburn hair flew in all directions. "I am eleven years old. And I plan to live to be twelve!"

So J.J. and Gracie ran circles around Cassie and Chester. Ever since her wild, runaway ride at the fair, Cassie had preferred to hold Chester to a poky snail's pace.

"Remember what happened at the fair? No way will I ride Chester without all of the proper equipment. I am definitely holding on," Cassie sputtered. "If I didn't, I'd be in that mud puddle by now." She pointed to the middle of the ring, where a recent rainstorm had left its mark.

From the kitchen door of the Holbrooks' house, Cassie's mother called. "J.J. Graystone, I'm not planning on taking you to the hospital tonight. Please use a bridle, at least!"

Cassie smiled with an "I-told-you-so" kind of look. J.J. scrunched her nose at Cassie.

For added effect, she poked out the tip of her tongue and crossed her eyes. Then she smiled at Mrs. Holbrook and said, "Okay Mrs. H., I will."

"Satisfied?" J.J. teased Cass. Then she dismounted and got the bridle that was hanging on the gate. Gracie accepted the bit into her mouth with a bit of coaxing. J.J. slid the head strap easily over the mare's attentive ears, then grabbing a tuft of Gracie's mane, J.J. leapt onto her mare's back again.

"I really don't mind the rules," said J.J., gathering the reins.

"I'm glad we can ride together!" said Cassie. "I'll learn a lot from you, J.J. And just look at Chester! You can tell that he likes having Gracie as his steady girl-friend."

The girls giggled, as they watched chunky Chester and graceful Gracie rub noses. What a funny, odd couple they made! The girls clucked to their horses and they walked their animals around the house and the new barn, up to the main road and back to the practice ring. In the light of the setting sun, they could see the cows resting and chewing their cud beneath the sprawling oak tree.

An evening breeze began to blow softly through the trees. It freshened the girls' moist, hot faces. Even the horses seemed to enjoy the breeze, since the flies couldn't land on their faces.

J.J. had fallen silent again, as her favorite daydream flooded her mind. "What are you thinking about?" Cassie asked gently.

J.J. thought a long moment before she spoke. "Well,

just suppose we lived a long time ago out west. You know, even before the west became part of the United States. If I were *Nascha* the Navajo maiden princess, who would you be?"

"Gee, I don't know," said Cassie, confused by the strange question.

"Oh, come on. Who would you be?"

With a glint in her eye, it was evident that Cassie had an idea. "Let's see, if you were a beautiful Navajo princess, I would probably be Clarabelle, the sun-burned pioneer girl. You would be dressed in your fine beaded animal skin dress, gliding across the prairie on Gracie. And there I'd be, bumping along in a rickety old covered wagon behind Chester!"

J.J. laughed. "I can just see you now in a sunbonnet, and poor Chester pulling a covered wagon!"

At the thought, both girls burst into a fresh round of laughter. Then J.J. said, "But really, get serious, Cass. Can't you see how romantic it would be to live that life? We would be as free as eagles!"

"But we're free now," said Cassie. "No thanks. I don't want to be a pioneer girl. Too much work! Can you imagine no running water and no electricity? I think it's better to live in the present day."

"Maybe," said J.J., her voice trailing off.

Then Cassie began to understand. "Whenever you are thinking of your Grandmother, you get that far-away look in your eyes."

J.J. closed her eyes. A familiar ache rose in her heart, as she remembered the hugs of a woman with sun-dried skin and kind, mysterious, indigo eyes much like her own.

"I know I do," she replied. "I wish I could see Grandmother."

For a long moment, the girls fell silent. A whippoor-will moaned his sad birdcall from a distant tree branch across the pasture.

Cassie spoke first. "Are you sorry that you moved here to Misty Falls?"

J.J. studied her friend's concerned hazel eyes. "Oh Cass, you know how much I love living here in Georgia with you. It is just so far away from my clan."

"Clan?" asked Cassie.

"Yes. You know, my family. It would be great to see all of my aunts, uncles, cousins, and Grandmother Teresa. You know, I was five when I left the Navajo Reservation. I can't remember many of the family members that my mother talks about. I would like to know them. But most of all, I miss my grandmother."

"I don't blame you," said Cassie, stroking Chester's neck. "My whole family lives here in Misty Falls. I can't imagine living far away from them."

"You understand everything," J.J. said gratefully. "See? If God really does work everything out for the best for those who love Him, He must have moved me here, so that we could be best friends."

J.J., Navajo Princess

Cassie smiled tenderly. She glanced toward the row of trees along the creek bank at the far edge of the pasture. "We need to have a chat on Talking Rock," said Cassie. "Come on."

She leaned over from Chester's back to unlatch the gate. The horses with their two riders flat-walked toward the creek to the girls' private talking spot.

For a while, they rode in silence. Then J.J. exclaimed, "You know what? It's too quiet!"

In a sudden rush of mischief, J.J. squeezed her legs against her mare's sides and yelled with glee, "*Nascha*, the Navajo princess, rides again! Last one to Possum Creek is a rotten egg!"

In a flash, Gracie's red and silver mane flew fiercely into the breeze. J.J. felt her own braided mane of dark hair sailing as well. Off Gracie galloped toward Possum Creek, with Cassie and Chester trailing after the Navajo Princess.

Over the drumming of hooves, J.J. could barely hear Cassie calling, "Hey, wait a second. I wasn't ready!" She glanced behind her. Cassie was trying to catch up, but Chester refused to move faster than an easy lope.

When Cassie arrived at the creek, J.J. was so amused that she couldn't hide her smile. She had already taken off Gracie's bridle and was letting her mare dip into the cool waters from a nearby natural spring for a drink. "What took you so long?" she teased. "How dare you keep Princess *Nascha* waiting!"

Cassie dismounted and put her hands on her hips. Then she flatly replied, "Ha, ha, very funny. You know Chester's short little legs can't keep up with the speed queen here." Gracie nickered softly, as if she knew the girls were talking about her.

J.J. and Cassie climbed onto their favorite resting spot, a boulder that jutted into the creek bed. They had named it "Talking Rock." Talking Rock was a place where they could talk and be undisturbed even when Cassie's little cousin Petey was over for a visit. Boys were never allowed on Talking Rock, not even Iggy Potts.

As they watched the waters rush over the rocky creek bed, Cassie nudged J.J. "J.J., aren't you ever going to tell me why you and your mother moved here, all the way from Arizona? I mean, I know your parents divorced and all. But you can tell me more if you want to."

J.J. paused. She had never spoken of some things before to Cassie or anyone. But she was feeling quite grown up lately and wanted to confide in her best friend. Finally she responded slowly.

"Well, as you know, my mother and father were unhappy together when I was little. My dad was gone a lot. When he was around, I was sort of afraid of him. I stayed with my grandmother in her hogan, while my mom worked and studied at school."

"What exactly is a hogan?" asked Cassie, her hazel

eyes wide with curiosity.

"It's a little like a cabin, only it's built in a circle. Mom says that a hogan's door always faces the east, so that the Navajo family can greet the sun every morning. All I remember is my grandmother in her long skirt. I remember how she leaned over the old stove, making fry bread. She always let me eat it with honey for breakfast and again at supper, along with corn and other vegetables."

"Sounds yummy," said Cassie.

"Oh, it is," said J.J. "Mom makes it sometimes. You'll have to come over and try it."

Cassie's freckles squished together as she crinkled her forehead. "So, I still don't know why you moved to Georgia," she said.

J.J. felt awkward and a little puzzled about how to answer. "I don't know. Mom doesn't talk about it much. I think she wants to protect me."

"Have you asked her about it?" Cassie asked anxiously.

"Yes," said J.J., gazing deeply into the rushing creek water. "I think that Mom doesn't want to say anything bad about my father. All I know is that she worked very hard on the reservation to support us. She took art classes at the Navajo Community College."

"Wow," said Cassie, "so that explains why your apartment is full of colorful paintings and sculptures. Your mom is really talented."

"Yes, she is, and smart, too!" J.J. replied proudly. "Mom has said that she wanted a better life for us, and that is why we moved. You see, a professor at the college recommended Mom for a job in Atlanta. That's how she came to work at the Children's Metropolitan Art Museum. And so we moved to Misty Falls."

Cassie grinned. "That's when I met you in Miss Bean's kindergarten class!"

"Exactly," said J.J. "You were my first friend in my new home state. Remember when we got in trouble for painting mud on the park bench at recess?"

Cassie giggled. "Yes, Miss Bean made us go back outside and clean it up. We were so muddy for the rest of the day."

J.J. laughed. "Mom wasn't very happy with me when I got home from school that day. I was mad at Mom for scolding me. I felt sure that Grandmother Teresa would have understood, though."

"You must have felt very sad leaving your grandmother," said Cassie.

J.J. replied softly. "I still write to her every week. Before we send it, Mom has to translate it into the Navajo language."

"Does she write back?" asked Cassie hopefully.

"Yes. She sends me tiny dried flowers from the canyon. Mom translates her letters for me. I know some Navajo words, but I can't remember many. It's a very difficult language.

"Anyway," continued J.J., "Mom still sends money each month to Grandmother. That is why I almost had to sell Gracie. Grandmother is lonely and is getting too old to care for the sheep herself now, so she has to hire helpers."

"Your poor grandmother," said Cassie. Her voice trailed off. Then she asked, "J.J., are you glad you live in Misty Falls now?"

J.J. took Cassie's face in her hands and spoke firmly. "I love Misty Falls! It is home to me now."

Cassie beamed. "I'm glad. I can't imagine what it would be like here without you."

J.J. smiled. She pulled off her shoes and socks, swished the creek water with her toes, and sighed dreamily. "Someday when I grow up, I will visit the land of my clan. Mom has taught me how important family is to the Navajo people. And she doesn't say much about it, but I can tell she misses her sisters and brothers and Grandmother Teresa, too. I don't even know what having a real father is like."

"I really can't imagine how that feels," said Cassie. "You know how close my dad and I are. I'll share him with you if you want!"

"Oh, I think he's the best," said J.J. as she hugged Cassie. "Thanks, Cassie. I'm a lucky girl to know such a great family."

Cassie thought and thought. Finally she said, "Why don't you go for a visit to the Navajo Reservation?

There's still a little time before school starts. You could see your grandmother and all your clan."

"I asked my mom at the beginning of summer, but she says we can't afford the trip. Besides, a visit is just a visit. It will not be the same as living there. Mother worries about Grandmother Teresa now that she is getting older. If only my grandmother and I were together…"

Cassie thought for a moment. Then her face brightened. "You know, Dad is talking about taking our family out west next summer. Maybe you could come too!"

"That would be great!" said J.J. She felt like smiling and crying at the same time. "But that is still a whole year away. Oh Cassie, do you really think I could go with you and your family? Who would take care of the farm? Who would take care of Gracie and Chester?"

"I don't know. But if we start praying now, God will have lots of time to work it out," said Cassie. "Don't worry."

"Let's pray right now," said J.J., feeling hopeful. She didn't know quite what to ask for. So sitting with their legs crisscrossed on Talking Rock, the girls held hands, bowed their heads, and began to have a conversation with God. J.J. liked how Cassie talked directly to Jesus Christ. Cassie asked God for his help in making J.J.'s dream come true.

But J.J. wasn't sure exactly what her dream was. She just knew that she missed her grandmother, and that the ache in her heart wouldn't go away.

J.J., Navajo Princess

2

By the time the girls made their way back to the barn to untack the horses, the sky was coal black and shimmering with stars. Cassie's little black and white dog, Opie, barked at the door as the girls entered the barn. They could hear the voices of Cassie's parents, brothers, and sisters chattering in the Holbrook kitchen.

"Oops, I think we're late for dinner," said Cassie, grinning as she brushed out Chester's black and white coat more quickly than usual.

J.J. wiped down Gracie with an old towel and brushed her. She gave Gracie and Chester each a scoop of grain and a fat flake of hay. While they ate, Cassie filled their buckets with water and added fresh straw bedding to their stalls.

The girls washed their hands and let them drip dry as they ran across the lawn to the back door. Opie greeted them with his friendly doggy "smile."

"Mmm," said J.J., "Your mom has been baking peach pie."

"Didn't you know?" Cassie teased, "Dessert is the most important food group at our house!" The girls laughed as they parked their dirty shoes on the back porch and entered the cheerful kitchen. A chorus of friendly hellos greeted the pair.

At the table, Cassie's parents, her brother Jeff, and her sisters Greta and Pat were already busy eating and talking together. Even Sid, who had his own apartment now, had joined them for dinner. J.J. was grateful to see two more places set at the table. She was hungry enough to eat a whole pie by herself!

Mr. Holbrook finished swallowing his last bite of mashed potatoes and gravy and said, "Here are the slowpokes! Welcome, J.J. Hi, Munchkin. You look like two tired puppies. Pull up a couple of chairs."

"Thank you, sir," said J.J. politely, as she sat between Cassie's big sisters, Greta and Pat. Eating at Cassie's house was always so much fun, and so delicious. J.J. felt like a regular member of the family.

"Sorry we're late," said Cassie, sliding in next to Jeff. "Any fried chicken left, or did Jeff eat it all?"

Jeff winked and bit off another chunk of chicken from his drumstick before answering. "I left a crumb or two," he mumbled. Then he smiled at J.J. "Cassie doesn't get any. But don't worry, I saved you a big piece."

Sid shook his head and grinned. "Don't pay any attention to him, J.J. He has a bottomless pit for a stomach."

"It's all that football practice," said Pat, the oldest of the Holbrook daughters. "During cheerleading practice today, I saw Jeff running the track, doing all those warm-up exercises, tackling guys bigger than himself, and running for touchdowns all afternoon."

"And weight training," said Jeff, with his mouth full.

Greta agreed. "With the high school football season starting soon, Jeff just about doubles his appetite just so that he can keep building his strength for the season."

"I'd better fry more chicken next time," said Mrs. Holbrook. "But Jeff has been like this ever since he was a baby. What a good little eater he was."

"Uh-oh," said Mr. Holbrook. "I feel a baby story coming on."

"Aw, Mom, not again," protested Jeff.

"But you were so cute," said Mrs. Holbrook, "messy, but cute! I remember when you first insisted on taking the baby spoon from my hand and feeding yourself mashed potatoes and strained carrots. I thought I'd never get it all cleaned out of your ears and hair."

As everyone laughed and teased Jeff, Mrs. Holbrook had another inspiration from the past. "And that night you finished a whole jar of toddler peas and then kissed Pat right on the mouth. Oh, that was so cute."

"Please don't bring me into this," said Pat, rolling her eyes.

Mrs. Holbrook got up from the table. "Now where did I put Jeff's baby photo album? I captured the scene in a great picture."

"That's okay, Mom," said Jeff, red-faced. Everyone laughed except Jeff. But the twinkle in his eye told J.J. that he was amused, too. That's what she liked about the Holbrook family—they had so much fun together.

Mrs. Holbrook gave up looking for the photo album. "Alright, Jeff, you have your wish. I'll get your plates, girls. I thought it was best to keep them hidden and warm in the microwave."

"Thank you, Mrs. H.," said J.J. Gratefully, she paused and silently thanked God for her food. She also thanked Him for the hope of someday being with Grandmother Teresa again. Right now, she would enjoy Cassie's family.

"Dad," said Cassie, between sips of milk, "are we still going to the Grand Canyon next summer?"

As soon as she heard Cassie's question, J.J. nearly choked on her milk. Her stomach was suddenly being attacked by a bunch of nervous butterflies, and it began to flutter with excitement. She hoped Cassie knew what she was doing.

"Funny you should ask about our vacation next summer," said Mr. Holbrook, glancing at his wife.

J.J., Navajo Princess

"Honey, Don and I went by the Auto Club office and picked up some information so we can start planning early. So Cassie, to answer your question, we've decided to take your Uncle Don's camper. The camper is large enough to hold us all. Aunt Mary, Uncle Don, and Petey will go along with us."

"Oh, how wonderful!" exclaimed Mrs. Holbrook. "My sister and I will be able to catch up with each other!"

But Cassie's face had turned a pale white. "Petey's going? Oh no! That will ruin everything!" J.J. understood. That meant Cassie would be babysitting.

"Why Cassie!" said Mrs. Holbrook. "You mustn't say such things. Petey is a fine little boy. He just has a lot of energy."

J.J. held her breath to hear what her friend would say next.

Then Cassie did it. She blurted, "But J.J. and I were going to have such a good time together. Now Petey has ruined it before we even get started!"

"J.J.? " stammered Mrs. Holbrook. "Is there a little plot in the works that your father and I don't know about, Cassie Marie?"

J.J. felt her face flush hot. She felt embarrassed that Cassie was inviting her on the trip before she had asked her parents. J.J.'s hands were so shaky, that she dropped her fork on the floor.

"Oops, I'll get your fork for you, J.J.," said Cassie.

But she and J.J. both dove under the table to pick up the fork.

"Why did you do that, Cassie?" whispered J.J. "I don't want to intrude on your family vacation."

"You're not intruding. It was my idea. I'm sorry, J.J. The words just came out! I'll explain, don't worry."

But J.J. was worried. It must have seemed to Cassie's parents that she had invited herself on the Holbrooks' family trip!

Jeff protested, "Hey, if Cassie gets to take a friend, why can't I?"

Before Greta and Pat could chime in, Mr. Holbrook held up his hand. "Hold it, hold it, I said we were taking a camper, not Air Force One. We won't have room for your army of friends. Now Munchkin, what's this all about?"

J.J. could tell that Cassie was trying to buy some time. First, she cleared her throat, then she folded her napkin neatly beside her plate of chicken bones.

"Well," Cassie began slowly, "you see, J.J.'s grandmother and many members of her family live in Arizona, on the Navajo Reservation."

"Oh, how interesting," said Mrs. Holbrook. She reached across the table and patted J.J. on the shoulder. "Do you see them often, dear?"

J.J. couldn't find her voice. She just smiled shyly, stared at her plate, and shook her head "no."

Cassie smiled and continued. "J.J. hasn't seen her

family, even her grandmother who took care of her, since she moved to Misty Falls."

"Oh, how sad," said Mrs. Holbrook, giving that pleading look to her husband. "Joe, would you step into the family room with me for a moment? I want to have a word with you."

Mr. Holbrook's eyes twinkled as he got up from the table. Before he left the table, he winked and said, "Honey. I know what you are thinking. I am thinking the same thing. We'll be right back."

While Mr. and Mrs. Holbrook talked quietly in the living room, Cassie squeezed J.J.'s arm. J.J.'s head was spinning with thoughts like running into the open arms of Grandmother Teresa outside the old hogan; like meeting her cousins, who had been too young for her to know very well when she lived on the Reservation; like exploring the canyon where she used to help Grandmother herd sheep.

When Cassie's parents returned to the table, Mr. Holbrook grinned broadly. "That settles it. J.J., we will be traveling to Arizona next June. That's about ten months away. We hope that you can come along with us. That is, if your mother approves."

J.J.'s heart nearly burst with joy. "Oh Mr. H., Mrs. H., everybody, I just can't thank you enough! Let's ask my mother tonight when she comes to pick me up. Thank you, thank you!"

Greta and Pat looked at each other and then hugged

J.J. "We're glad you can go on our summer vacation with us! It will be fun to visit a Navajo Reservation," said Greta, poking J.J.'s arm. "Looks like I'll have two kid sisters next summer."

J.J. smiled. She liked the idea of being a sister to Cassie, Greta, and Pat.

Just then, Opie started to bark, announcing that a car was pulling up in the driveway. J.J. looked out the window. "It's my mom," she said, excitedly. "Cassie, I'd better get my shoes and go out to the car right away. I can't wait to ask her."

Mrs. Holbrook held up her hand. "Oh, Cassie, J.J., do ask her to come in. We'll have peach pie in the family room and talk about our vacation plans for next summer."

In no time, J.J.'s mom had joined the Holbrooks in the family room. As J.J. helped serve the pie, her heart pounded out a rhythm while her mind sang, *Grandmother, I'm coming! Grandmother, I'm coming! Wait for me! I'm coming!*

"Did you have a good day at the children's museum?" asked Mr. Holbrook politely. "That sounds like very interesting work."

"Oh it is," said Ms. Graystone. "But today was challenging. Our featured exhibit for next month had to cancel at the last minute. Now I don't know what I'm going to feature for the children who visit the museum next month. It's a key exhibit, because school will be starting soon, and we have many groups scheduled to come and see it. I hope I can find a replacement by then."

"That is a problem," said Mrs. Holbrook. "You have quite a lot of responsibility at the museum, don't you?"

"More than I care to have at times, I must admit," chuckled Ms. Graystone. "But I love my work. Anyway, how was the day on the farm?"

"Great," said Cassie. "J.J. is a wonderful horseback rider. She is so brave and talented."

"And Carol," added Mrs. Holbrook, "talent and courage are wonderful qualities, but she is also such a sweetheart. Not only do I enjoy her in my Sunday School class, but she is like one of the family around here."

J.J. blushed and thanked Mrs. Holbrook for the kind compliment. "I like spending time here too," she said.

"I am glad to hear that." Ms. Graystone, still in her business suit from a day of working at the children's museum, gave her daughter an approving smile. Then she took a bite of her pie and added, "Thank you for boarding J.J.'s horse for us and allowing J.J. to come over so often. I know how much she loves being with Cassie. I believe the good Lord Jesus gave us your friendship."

J.J. stole a look at Cassie. They both wriggled with anticipation. J.J. was already beginning to wonder how she could wait until next summer for the westward journey to begin!

Mr. Holbrook entered the conversation. "Carol, our family is going out west to Arizona next June. Now I know that's nearly a year away, but we'd like to take J.J. with us. We understand the two of you have family out there. We're taking a large camper, and there's plenty of room for J.J."

"Oh? I see," said J.J.'s mom. Her dark eyes examined J.J.'s dark blue ones. J.J. felt a strange chill flow through her. She tried to smile, but she knew instantly that her mom didn't feel comfortable hearing this.

Mrs. Holbrook chimed in. "Oh Carol, we would just love for J.J. to travel with us. As a matter of fact, you are more than welcome to join us, if you can take the time off from work."

J.J. held her breath, waiting. The room was so quiet. She could hear an owl softly hooting outside a mile away.

Mom, J.J. thought to herself, *why don't you answer?* Everyone in the room seemed to grow suddenly uncomfortable with the silence, especially J.J.

Finally, setting down her plate of half-eaten pie, Ms. Graystone spoke. "Well. Thank you for dessert and your kind invitation. J.J. and I will discuss this at home. I will have to think about it."

"Oh certainly," said Mrs. Holbrook. "There's plenty of time."

"Excuse us, but we must get going now. J.J., it's quite late, and I have an early meeting in the morning at the museum. Goodnight, everyone, and thank you again."

"Goodnight," the Holbrooks called in hushed unison.

"I'll talk to you tomorrow," said J.J. to Cassie.

"Call me," said Cassie with a friendly wave.

J.J. and her mother stepped outside. J.J. looked back toward the house and waved. Then she tried to catch up to her mom. Ms. Graystone was walking so fast that she couldn't keep up.

As she slid into the front seat of the car, J.J. asked, "Mom, are you upset? What? Why?" J.J. couldn't think of how to express her questions.

"Not now," said Ms. Graystone, starting the car. "We will discuss this at home."

J.J. knew not to argue. As her mother drove, J.J. closed her eyes. She felt her heart deflate like a balloon. There wasn't really any need to "discuss this at home." She already knew her mother's answer. She would not be allowed to go with the Holbrooks next summer to visit her native land. She would not get to visit Grandmother Teresa. She wouldn't be allowed to visit the cousins, aunts, and uncles that she couldn't even remember. And she wouldn't see her father, whom she hadn't seen since they left the reservation.

But why? Would she ever know?

There were no tears in Jennifer Joy to cry. No joy

either. Just a strange, empty feeling that she couldn't understand.

J.J., Navajo Princess

3

J.J. wondered if her mom would ever say anything more about the Holbrooks' trip. In the stiff silence, the short ride back to their apartment seemed to drag on forever. J.J. wished she could sit on Talking Rock with Cassie right now. But perhaps there was nothing left to talk about.

As her mom turned off the engine, J.J. unfastened her seat belt. She was a little surprised to hear her mother speak. "Go inside J.J., and wash up. Get ready for bed, then we will talk."

"Okay," said J.J. She felt lonely and cold, as if she were having a strange dream. *Would the dream have a happy ending?* She wondered.

As quickly as she could, J.J. showered and put on fresh pajamas. She turned her bedside lamp on the low setting and sat on her bed.

Her yellow and white cat, Frisco, jumped onto the bed and began to purr. He rubbed against her arm until she held him in her lap. "You silly old fur trap," J.J. whispered.

J.J. always talked to Frisco as if he were a real person. In fact, he was easier to talk to than most people, except Cassie. "Oh Frisco, at least you, Gracie, and Mama are my family. But I miss my grandmother. I don't know my other family members at all, or at least not very well. Can you tell me why Mama is acting so strangely? Why doesn't she want me to visit our family?"

Frisco only purred louder. He leaned his furry head against J.J.'s fingers for more intense head rubbing. At first, J.J. didn't notice that her mother was standing at the bedroom door. She had been there, listening to J.J.'s questions. She gasped when she realized Mama had heard her thoughts.

As her mother silently walked across the colorful, worn, woolen rug that Grandmother had weaved when J.J. was born, J.J. noticed that she was carrying a great, fat book. J.J. had never seen the book before.

She scooted over and made a place for Mama to sit. Frisco rubbed against Mama's arm, which cradled the book as though it were a precious new baby. Although the book's binding had been made of tough, tanned hide, it was well worn from much use.

"What is this book?" J.J. asked timidly. "Is there something you want to tell me?"

"It is alright to ask such questions, Jennifer Joy." Mom touched J.J.'s long black hair. "My *Nascha*, my little wise owl. The Navajo name your grandmother gave you suits you very well. You are like the little owl whose eyes see all, even in the dark of night."

J.J.'s heart beat faster, as she saw tears form in her mother's round, dark eyes. Mom had never cried before—at least in front of J.J.

"Listen, J.J. You are twelve years old, old enough to hear. I will tell you why I'm struggling to decide whether to let you return to our homeland for a visit."

J.J. listened intently as her mother spoke.

"When I was your age, I never dreamed I would leave my home someday," Mom began. "We Navajo people are very close. As a people, we cherish family. My mother and father loved me. My aunts and uncles loved me—they were like extra mothers and fathers. My cousins were like brothers and sisters. We ate together, celebrated together, and lived close together. It was the way I wanted you to grow up, too."

Mom's voice was tender, and sometimes she had to stop to take a deep breath. J.J. reached out and touched her hand. "Go on, Mama. I'm listening."

"The Navajo people have many customs, many traditions. I was taught to speak Navajo. I grew up knowing our native customs in the old hogan, where Grandmother Teresa still lives. I went to school and took pride in who I was as a Navajo girl. I have taught many of the customs to you. You have the spirit of the Navajo, as I do. God made the Navajo people strong, brave, and free. You can be very proud of your people."

J.J. meant to keep silent, but she forgot. Instead, she blurted, "So why were you not pleased that Cassie's family wants me to go on this trip? Especially since I would be able to visit our family. I would get to see Grandmother! Is that wrong?"

Her mother paused, then said, "J.J., there is something else you need to know. I was married to your father before I became a Christian. For the first time, I heard about Jesus when a missionary and his wife came to teach us Bible stories. In my heart, I knew that the Bible stories were true, because they are from God's very own words. I became a Christian."

Mama stopped for a moment, then bravely continued. J.J. could tell that this was difficult for her to say. "When your father found out that I was a Christian, he became angry. Some of our clan felt that this Jesus was a threat to the Navajo beliefs."

"Oh, Mama!" J.J. cried. "I believe in Jesus, too."

"Yes, my little one. When you were very small, I decided to start teaching you the truth of God's Word. Your heart was very open to Him. His Word is for all people everywhere, old and young alike. His love is for the Native American people, too," her mom said with strength in her voice.

"My father did not agree?" J.J. asked. Tiny goose bumps popped up on J.J.'s skin, and she shivered.

"He was very angry. He didn't understand and said

some bad things. When you were still a baby, he wanted to take you away from me, to keep you from hearing the good news of Jesus Christ. I wanted to protect you. So you lived safe and sound with Grandmother in the old hogan, where I grew up."

"Why was my father so angry at Jesus?" J.J. asked. She hung her head, so that her hair might hide the tears in her eyes.

"Oh, I am not sure. He was drunk sometimes. That was when he would be most angry. I want you to know something, J.J. I love your father and pray for him every day. I miss being a wife to him. But I could not stay with him, because we were in danger. He was so angry. I had to protect my child. I had to make a good life for my little *Nascha*. So we moved to Atlanta, where you and I could worship Jesus and you could grow up happy, joyful, and free."

J.J.'s head was swimming. She was glad to know the truth, but equally sad. "Is my father still angry?" she whispered.

Mom sighed. "I do not know for sure. Grandmother doesn't say much about him. She said once that he tried not to drink alcohol anymore. He works at a trading post in Flagstaff. That is all I know."

"Mama, does our clan know that Jesus is God's Son?"

"They have heard it. Some believe and some do not. Some of our people are not trusting of what they feel is the 'white man's religion.' A pastor there is trying to help them understand that God sent His Son Jesus for all the people of the world."

Then Mama's voice became more cheerful. "But *Nascha*, do not be sad. More and more of our clan are believing the missionaries. Your Aunt Joan wrote to me last week with good news. Some of your cousins attended Vacation Bible School and accepted Jesus Christ as Lord and Savior. Aunt Joan is a Christian, too!"

"Oh, Mom, that's great!" J.J. exclaimed. "I want to know my cousins and my Aunt Joan. May I write to them?"

Mom smiled. "I have an even better idea. My sister Joan has email. You and her children, Cole and Tera, can write to each other."

Then a thought occurred to J.J. It was such a happy, hopeful thought that she wanted to share it with her mother. So she did. "Maybe by next summer, God will make it safe for me to visit Grandmother and all our clan. Even my father."

Mom seemed to hold her breath for a moment. Then she tweaked J.J.'s nose and said, "Perhaps my little owl is right. She can be very wise, you know."

New hope lit up J.J.'s eyes. Then, curious, she glanced at the mysterious book her mother was holding. She could wait no longer for the answer to her next question.

"Mama, please tell me what is in the book!"

As Ms. Graystone studied her daughter's wondering eyes, she couldn't help smiling. "Oh J.J., I believe sometimes I am looking at myself as a girl again when I look at you!" she exclaimed with pleasure. Then she gave J.J. a closer look. "And yet, I look again, and there is Grandmother Teresa in your eyes. You have her spirit." Mama paused, then hugged the great book. J.J. could smell its musty leather fragrance. "I've been keeping this for you."

"Open the book, Mama, please! I can't wait anymore," begged J.J. excitedly. "What is inside?"

Mama started to open the book. Then she said, "I have a better idea. Why don't you open the book yourself?" She tried to hand the book to J.J., but Frisco was in the way. "Come now, silly cat, you've had enough petting. Get off the bed. Shoo!"

"Mee-owww," complained Frisco, as he stared with disdain at his owners. J.J. laughed at him for acting so insulted. Frisco curled up on top of a basket filled with J.J.'s laundry and cleaned his coat with his long, rough, pink tongue.

Finally J.J.'s Mom placed the book in J.J.'s lap so that its weight rested heavily against her upper legs. J.J.'s heart seemed to skip a beat with all the excitement.

The pages were covered in plastic for protection. On the first page was J.J.'s baby picture and the words:

Adventures in Misty Falls

Jennifer Joy Graystone
Traditional Navajo Name: Nascha ("owl")
Born to Tahoma and Carol Kai Graystone
Flagstaff, Arizona

"This is your history, J.J.," said her mom softly. "It is the history of your clan and of the Navajo people. I began making it for you shortly after you were born. Now you will know who you are. Someday, you can show this book to your children and grandchildren."

"Me? A grandmother?" asked J.J., surprised by the prospect of being a grandmother someday. "I can't imagine being that old!"

Mama laughed and hugged J.J. "Don't worry, neither can I!"

"Thank you, Mama," J.J. said. She only called her mom "Mama" when she had that special, loving feeling. Tonight was such a time. She pointed to one of the many sketches and paintings in the book. "Did you paint this?"

"Yes," said her mom, "it is the great Seal of the Navajo Nation. When we see the seal, it reminds us to be proud of our people and our customs."

"The colors are so bright and alive!" said J.J., as she studied the seal carefully. She smiled when she turned the page. There was a photograph of J.J. as a young child at her mother's side, learning how to paint.

"You are quite an artist, too," said J.J.'s mother. "Look, here, at this one. You drew that picture shortly after we moved to Georgia. Remember?"

Surprised, J.J. exclaimed with a laugh, "It's Gracie, when she was still a yearling! Look, I drew her legs off-kilter."

"Very good for a young artist," said Mom.

The book was filled with pages and pages of keepsakes and photographs of her parents, grandparents, cousins, aunts, and uncles. There were several of Mom's sketches of the landscape on the Navajo Reservation. Best of all, J.J. discovered photos of herself with Grandmother, as they tended sheep together and ground herbs for cooking on the big flat stone beside the hogan.

Learning so much at once made J.J.'s head throb with excitement. She rubbed her eyes and closed the book. Kissing her mother's darkly tanned cheek; she hugged the book tightly to her chest. "I'll treasure my book—always!"

Then J.J. began to look at the pages she had not yet seen. "Whoa, now, time for lights out," objected her mom. "There's plenty of time tomorrow."

J.J. groaned. "But I'm not a bit sleepy. Can't I stay up a little longer? See, here is a picture of my father I have not seen."

She studied the faded black and white photograph carefully. Her father looked young and handsome in a dark jacket and jeans. His black hair was thick and blowing in the wind...

"He was quite handsome, don't you agree?" asked Mama with a sigh. Then her facial expression changed into that "you'd-better-do-as-I-say" look. "Jennifer Joy…"

J.J. sighed, closed the book again, and placed it by her side. As she sank deep into covers and lay her head on the soft pillow, she kept smiling. "Yes, ma'am. I'm going to sleep now. But tomorrow, I'm going to email my cousins!"

As usual, crawling under the covers was Frisco's signal to join J.J. on the bed once again. J.J. snuggled tightly with him for a while as she tingled with wonder. Finally, she understood more about who she was. She felt prouder than ever to be a Native American, a Navajo. And she was prouder than ever to belong to Jesus Christ.

In the moonlight that danced against her curtains in the open-window breeze, J.J. began to pray. "Dear Jesus, now I understand at least a little bit about the reasons why Mom took me away from the reservation. You were watching out for us, even when I didn't understand. Help me to learn all I can about Your love, so that I can return to Arizona with lots of love for my aunts, uncles, and cousins, and for my grandmother and my father."

Frisco's purring grew softer and the room fell into a peaceful silence. *Nascha*, the Navajo Princess, had finally fallen asleep…

J.J., Navajo Princess

4

Early the next morning, the ringing phone awakened J.J. She opened her eyes halfway. Frisco yawned and stretched his yellow paws. Trying to sit up, J.J. discovered she had fallen asleep hugging her Navajo treasure book.

"It's Cassie—for you, J.J.," Mom said from the phone in the hall. Mom pressed a button on the phone. "You're on the speaker phone, Cassie. J.J. is just getting up. She'll be with you in a moment."

"Oops! Did I call too early?" asked Cassie, as J.J. stumbled into the hall half-asleep. "Oh well, rise and shine, girlfriend! Nurse Trixie called my mother early this morning, and Robyn is bored stiff. I can't believe we haven't seen her in nearly a week! Trixie also said Hunter Harris will be there visiting Madison. It sounds like they are all terribly bored and need cheering up. We need to go over there today."

J.J. yawned and blinked her eyes. "That sounds like a good plan. Oh Cassie," she added, remembering last night's talk with her mom, "I have so much to tell you."

"Great," said Cassie. "I can't wait to see you. I've already taken care of the chores for the both of us today, so we can spend our whole day having fun."

"Really?" J.J. said in surprise. "You're the best, Cass. Did you even turn Gracie and Chester out in the pasture?"

"Yes," replied Cassie with amusement in her voice. "You should have seen them bucking and kicking and running around. I love to see them in the pasture after they've been closed up in the barn for a while. They are so playful! Oh, Mom is telling me to say that we'll be there to pick you up in a half hour. We're going to stop and get Iggy first."

J.J. happened to think of how to get home later. "Does my mom need to pick us up on the way home from work?" she asked.

"I'm way ahead of you," said Cassie. "My mother will stop by for us later. Hunter, Iggy, and you are all invited to come back to the farm afterward. Bring something to swim in, but not your best swimsuit. We're all going back to go swimming in the hole in Possum Creek. Dad is going to grill hamburgers. Okay, gotta go. See you in a half hour!"

"Make it an hour," said J.J., groggily. She wanted more time to explore her special book.

"You can hurry," argued Cassie.

"See you in thirty minutes."

J.J. smiled and shook her head. Cassie usually couldn't make a decision very easily. But once she was set on something, there was no turning back.

It was a good thing J.J. had showered the night before, or she could have never been ready in time. She slipped on some shorts, a colorful top, and her sandals, braided her hair quickly, and brushed her teeth. Looking around her room, she found a safe place to store her Navajo book. She tucked it carefully in the keepsake trunk Mom had made her out of cottonwood.

J.J. couldn't wait to tell Cassie what she had learned about herself, her family, and her Navajo heritage. But she would have to wait for the right time. She didn't want to just blurt it out.

Before she ran out to the car with Mrs. Holbrook, Iggy, and Cassie, J.J. hugged her mother. "Thank you, Mama," she said, as Ms. Graystone prepared for work. "I love you. Have a good day!"

In the car, Iggy greeted them with flash photography. His long, lanky legs seemed to have grown longer than ever, because he seemed to have trouble getting comfortable with his legs scrunched up in the backseat.

"Have you been growing again?" J.J. asked him with a yawn.

"As a matter of fact, I've grown an inch and a half this summer," Iggy said proudly. His red hair and freckles seemed to light up as he made the announcement.

Thanks to Iggy, J.J. was soon wide awake. He took lots of pictures of the girls and clowned around as usual. He seemed especially pleased with himself this morning.

"Hold onto your seats, girls! Nurse Trixie and I have a surprise for you!" he bragged.

"What are you talking about?" asked J.J.

"It's a secret," said Iggy, sniffing proudly. "A secret surprise. I can't tell. Sorry."

Cassie nearly exploded with impatience. "Come on Iggy. You know I hate it when you do this. Stop teasing us and tell us what your surprise is."

"It's not my surprise, exactly. You'll just have to wait and see," he said, wiggling his eyebrows up and down.

Cassie's sighs were more like huffs and puffs, but J.J. was so preoccupied by thoughts of her own that she really didn't feel too eager to learn what Iggy's surprise was.

Iggy's secret was just driving Cassie wild. She kept insisting on knowing. "I just hate secrets, unless they're my secrets, of course!" exclaimed Cassie.

"You'll find out when we get to New Hope Center," said Iggy. "For the last time, my lips are sealed."

J.J., Cassie, and Iggy walked into the lobby of New Hope Rehabilitation Center for Children, just as

Hunter was helping his little sister tie her shoelaces. While he tied them, Madison (Maddie, for short) tickled the back of his dark brown neck and twirled her black curls between her tiny fingers. J.J. noticed that Maddie giggled with glee anytime her big brother was around. She adored him.

"Hey, cut that out, Maddie!" said Hunter, signing the words to his deaf little sister so that she could understand. "Stop, please!"

Maddie giggled harder and kissed him on the nose. J.J. and Cassie doubled over laughing.

"She's so cute," said J.J., giving Maddie a friendly hug.

"Spoiled is more like it," said Hunter, rolling his chocolate-brown eyes. A little sheepishly, he admitted, "But you've gotta love her."

Just then, Nurse Trixie walked around the corner into the lobby. "Hi, y'all," said Trixie, in her pleasant southern accent.

"Hi y'all," said Iggy. He seemed to enjoy making fun of Nurse Trixie's accent. No one enjoyed it more than Trixie herself. But she faked a frown anyway.

"Hi," said Cassie. "Look, we brought the photographer."

"Hey," said Iggy. "Do you think the children would enjoy having a group picture made on the playground outside?"

"They would love it!" Trixie exclaimed. "Let me see.

They will all be coming to art class later this morning. We'll do it then."

"I'm ready," said Iggy, as he loaded film in his camera. "Guess what? Me and Nurse Trixie have a surprise for you—I mean, y'all."

Now it was Trixie's turn to tease Iggy back. "Okay, mister, that's 'Nurse Trixie and I,' not 'Me and Nurse Trixie.'"

"I stand corrected, ma'am," said Iggy, standing at attention.

"Where's the surprise?" asked J.J., curiously looking around. "In fact, where's Robyn?"

"Actually," said Nurse Trixie, "there are two surprises. Iggy doesn't know about one of them yet. I think you'll find them both in Robyn's room."

"Another surprise?" asked Iggy. "Come on, Trixie, you can tell your old pal, Iggy."

"Ha ha ha," said Cassie. "Mr. Know-it-all doesn't know so much anymore."

"The surprises are down there. I'll see y'all later," said Nurse Trixie, pointing down a long hallway. She grinned and took Maddie by the hand. "Miss Maddie will go with me for her hearing therapy session. Have a good time today. See you later for the group picture!"

They waved to Maddie and Trixie. Then they headed down the long hallway. The kids dashed to Robyn's door, which was covered with a new set of colorful stickers and brightly painted posters of flowers and birds.

Iggy knocked smugly. He seemed proud that he already knew at least one of the surprises that were in store. "It's me, Iggy," he announced. "They're here, Robyn. It's Hunter, Cassie, and J.J. Can we come in?"

"Sure—oh, wait a minute," chirped the cheerful little voice on the other side of the door. "I'll open the door for **you**!"

At first there were some thuds and thumps, then silence. J.J. wondered whether Robyn had fallen on her crutches. *What could she be doing in there? Should they check on Robyn, or call the nurse?* J.J. wondered.

5

"Are you alright?" asked J.J., as the others held their breath.

"May we come in, Robyn?" Iggy asked, shifting from one foot to the other.

After what seemed like forever, Robyn's door opened wide. J.J. couldn't believe her eyes. There was Robyn Alexa Morgan, with no walkers, wheelchair, crutches, or cane. Robyn was standing on her own. What's more, she was walking!

"I can't believe it," whispered Cassie. "Robyn, this is so wonderful!"

Robyn beamed and proclaimed, "Finally, after all those surgeries, I can walk all by myself! Following the car accident, no one expected me to ever walk again. And just look! I can twirl too! Dr. Ken is very proud of me."

She held her arms out to her sides in mid-air and sang, "Ta-da!" She twirled cautiously on her tiptoes, as her short blond hair tossed about.

J.J. squealed and clapped her hands. She and Cassie each gave Robyn a huge bear hug.

"Hurray!" shouted Hunter. "Way to go, girl. When did this happen?"

"Yesterday," said Robyn, smiling ear-to-ear. "Dr. Ken said my muscles are stronger, and I should walk without my crutches now. That will make my legs get even stronger. But that's not even the best part, I have another surprise."

The children were so eager to find out Robyn's second surprise that they started begging in chorus. Hunter, Iggy, Cassie, and J.J. all wanted to know Robyn's other secret.

"Yep," said Robyn. A twinkle in her blue eyes told all her friends how happy she was. "I'm going home this weekend! I'm going home to live with Aunt Felicia and Uncle Steve!"

"Oh, I hoped that was what it was!" exclaimed J.J.

"Wow!" said Iggy, as everyone sent up a whoop of celebration.

Cassie blinked her hazel eyes that were misting up with happiness for Robyn. "It's a miracle! How does it feel to be on your own two legs and getting ready to go home?" she asked excitedly.

"A little wobbly, but great!" said Robyn. "I can't wait to see my very own room in Aunt Felicia's gingerbread house."

The children looked at each other with puzzled

faces. "Gingerbread house?"

Robyn giggled. "Oh yes, that's what I call their stone cottage. From a distance, it looks like it's made of gingerbread cookies, like in *Hansel and Gretel.*"

Hunter's smile faded a little. Suddenly he seemed very concerned, even worried. "If you're not going to live at the New Hope Center any longer, does this mean you will be moving far away from Misty Falls?"

"Oh no, don't you remember? I'll be entering fifth grade at Misty Falls Elementary School. No more private tutors. I get to go to a real school! You guys will be right next door at the Middle School, but we will still see each other sometimes. We can email each other, too. And I'm sure I will be allowed to have visitors at my new home!"

J.J.'s face brightened. She was glad Robyn would be around this fall. Then J.J. had another thought. She was so excited that she spoke her thoughts aloud. "Email... I almost forgot! That's how I can find out more about my Navajo family. I'm going to write my cousins on the Navajo Reservation as soon as I get home. Mom won't mind letting me use her laptop computer and..."

Suddenly J.J. realized her friends were all staring at her. "Are you alright?" asked Cassie, looking concerned. "You were mumbling about something."

"What's on your mind, J.J.?" asked Iggy. "You can tell us."

"Oh, uh, nothing, maybe later," J.J. said, feeling her face flush.

Hunter patted J.J.'s shoulder. "Don't worry," he said. "After an hour or so with Maddie, I talk to myself too."

J.J. laughed. "I'm glad I'm not the only one!" she exclaimed cheerfully. She didn't want to just blurt out her own news right then. This was Robyn's moment.

Robyn poked Iggy with her elbow and shifted her eyebrows up and down. "Shall we show them—you know—our special secret?"

Iggy nodded and grinned.

"Another secret? Oh no," said Hunter.

Cassie squeezed J.J.'s arm. "Whatever it is, it can't be as great as Robyn's news."

"That's for sure!" said J.J.

Iggy agreed. "You're right. Our walking, talking, going-home Robyn is the best surprise. But this next surprise is one of a kind!"

As the kids stood up to leave, Maddie skipped into the room and took Robyn by the hand. She seemed to know what was going on already, because the little girl tugged at Robyn's hand insistently.

"Okay, Maddie, lead the way," said Cassie, placing her hands squarely on her hips. "Let's go. I can't stand the suspense of all these surprises and secrets!"

"I'm ready to know what this is all about," said J.J. "Can't you give us a hint?"

"We can't tell you," said Robyn. "We have to show you!"

J.J. could hardly tell that Robyn had been through so many surgeries to help her heal from the car accident. She was very quick, even nimble, without her crutches. And little Maddie skipped alongside her with lots of bounce.

"Hey, wait for me," yelled Iggy. "It's my secret too!" But Robyn and Maddie had already burst out the door into the sunshine.

J.J., Navajo Princess

6

"Come on, slowpokes!" squealed Robyn with delight. The tiniest ten-year-old that J.J. had ever met led the way along the huge, green lawn. Hunter, J.J., and Cassie followed Robyn and Maddie, while Iggy snapped pictures left and right with his trusty camera.

"Where are we going?" called Hunter, sprinting alongside the girls.

"That's the way to the petting zoo," Cassie said. "I found it that day we were here for the picnic. Do you suppose they have some new baby goats or something? Maybe that's the secret."

"I have no idea," said Hunter, gasping for breath, "but I think the photographer knows. Look, Iggy's taking a shortcut through the bushes."

J.J. caught a glimpse of Iggy's fiery red hair disappearing behind a wild grapevine, then she heard a yelp, a loud *kerthunk,* and then a splash. "What was that?"

Hunter started laughing. "I think Iggy's shortcut took him through the creek."

Cassie, J.J., and Hunter stopped trying to follow Robyn and Maddie. They had already lost them anyway.

"We'd better go check on Iggy," said Cassie, shaking her head of honey-auburn hair.

Pressing through the overgrown bushes, J.J. spotted a big hole just before they arrived at the creek. "Watch out, don't step in that." She pointed to the hole that was partly covered by leaves.

The three walked around the hole and stood by the creek bank. Sitting waist high in water was Iggy, with creek water dripping from his red curls. He was holding his camera high above his head, so that it wouldn't get wet.

After a while, Iggy spoke. "So J.J., where were you when I walked right into that hole and flipped head first into the creek?"

Everyone burst into laughter. They laughed so hard that tears rolled down their cheeks.

Robyn and Maddie appeared through the bushes on the opposite side of the creek. "What's up?" asked Robyn, then she saw Iggy. "Did you decide to take a swim?"

Iggy's deadpan expression looked so funny that everyone couldn't help but laugh. They were so consumed with Iggy's funny accident that they didn't notice what Maddie was doing. She had kicked off her sandals and was wading into the water.

When Hunter finally noticed, he waved his arms, trying to get his deaf little sister's attention. "No, Maddie, don't get wet," he said. "Robyn, get her hand, or she will jump all the way in! She loves water."

But it was too late. Little Maddie had joined Iggy in the water. Now they were both soggy. Iggy, who was a good swimmer, held Maddie's waist so that she wouldn't sink. Meanwhile, Maddie laughed and hugged Iggy around the neck.

"Nice day for a swim," said Iggy, without cracking a smile.

Maddie dipped her chocolate brown hand into the cool, clear water and splashed Iggy's pale freckled face.

"You two look so funny!" chuckled Hunter. Then he thought of something. "Hey, I should take your picture for a change, Iggy."

Suddenly, Maddie splashed her big brother with water too. "That does it!" he added, wading into the creek. Just as he reached out his hand for Maddie's, Hunter's foot slipped and into the creek he went.

J.J. looked at Cassie. Cassie looked at J.J., then they both looked across the creek at Robyn.

"Why wait until this afternoon to go swimming?" asked J.J., as she slipped off her sandals. "I'm ready to get wet!" With that, J.J. and Cassie waded into the creek, too. Hunter took Maddie to Robyn, who had stayed close to the creek's edge. There, the two smallest of the girls hunted for salamanders in shadowy places along the bank.

After a short but fierce splash fight, Iggy, J.J., Cassie, and Hunter looked around them. "Robyn and Maddie have disappeared again," observed Hunter.

Iggy waded out of the opposite side of the creek and disappeared. The rest of the soggy friends sloshed their way down the shady, wooded path toward the petting zoo.

Squish, squish, squish, splat. Squish, squish, squish, splat. They followed Robyn and Maddie's footprints in the soft dirt.

Cassie was obviously starting to worry. Her face was crinkled with concern. "What if Robyn and Maddie were to get lost?" she imagined out loud. Finally, she could stand it no longer. With all her might, she called "Ro-o-o-byn!"

Everyone listened for a response. And then came the reply in the distance. "Eeee—hawwwww!"

Hunter started to grin. "Ah-ha! Now I know what's going on. Maddie loves the animals in the petting zoo. Come on, everybody." He led the way down the path and into a clearing, where all sorts of little shelters and fences housed some very interesting animals.

In a fenced area stood Robyn, stroking the long neck of the funniest looking, light brown striped horse J.J. had ever seen.

"This is Rufus," said Robyn, rubbing his long floppy ears. "Guess what kind of animal he is! Don't tell them the answer, Iggy."

He had four legs, two floppy ears, and light brown stripes on his back and legs. He sort of looked like a horse, but he had a strange, short, stringy tail, and not much of a mane. The children all gathered around the strange-looking animal.

"Is it some sort of pony?" asked Cassie. By the way Cassie's nose was all scrunched up, J.J. could tell that Cassie knew she was wrong.

"Nope, guess again," Robyn said, giggling.

"A mule!" said Hunter. He seemed sure of it.

"Not even close," said Robyn, obviously enjoying her game.

"Well, it seems to be some sort of zebra," said J.J. "Judging from the faint brown stripes on his back."

Cassie looked at Hunter. "Have you ever seen anything like this before?"

"Never," said Hunter. "I've brought Maddie to the Center's petting zoo lots of times. We've seen emus, chickens, ducks, and pigs, but this is one really weird animal."

"Oh come on, Robyn, give us a hint!" J.J. exclaimed.

While Maddie patted Rufus' long black nose, Robyn proudly announced, "This, my friends, is a 'zedonk.'"

"A ze-what?" exclaimed Cassie.

"Oh come on, Robyn, there's no such animal."

"Correction," said Robyn. "There aren't many zedonks, but there are a few."

"Oh, I see," said J.J., "Rufus is half zebra and half donkey!"

"Right!" said Robyn. "My Aunt Felicia is shipping this little fellow to his owners, and they gave her permission to bring him out to our petting zoo for a little visit. Rufus has been here all week, entertaining the New Hope kids with his unusual looks."

"Wow," said Hunter. "The New Hope Center has a funny farm!"

Iggy laughed. "Good one, Hunter!" The boys gave each other a high-five hand slap.

Robyn explained. "Aunt Felicia says that the owners have been breeding zebras to donkeys. The result is a nice calm animal that can be ridden like a horse. See? He likes people. His owners will pick him up next week and take him to their petting zoo up north. I wish I could ride him. He's nice."

Cassie volunteered. "You can come to the farm and ride Chester sometime, if it's alright with your doctors and your aunt."

"Really? Thanks Cassie!" Robyn said, her eyes lighting up. "You know? Maybe I can ride sooner than I think. Now that I'm off crutches, nothing's going to hold me back."

While the children visited the animals, they each

selected their favorites. J.J. fell in love with two pygmy goats that hopped from one tree stump to another. Cassie liked holding a miniature potbellied pig. Hunter and Maddie liked Rufus best of all.

"I don't really have a favorite animal," said Robyn. "I like all the animals. Aunt Felicia found these for New Hope Center. She wanted us kids who are getting well to enjoy taking care of them."

Iggy really didn't much care about petting the animals. He just wanted to take pictures of them, even though he was still dripping wet.

J.J. was a little wet too, but she didn't mind. She was having fun. They fed the greedy ducks and chickens, the goats, the Vietnamese potbellied pig, and of course, Rufus, while Iggy used up three rolls of film.

Finally, Iggy checked his waterproof watch. "Uh-oh!" he exclaimed. "It's time for the group photograph of the children at New Hope. We've got to get back. Let's hurry! To the craft room, everyone!"

J.J. sighed as she followed the group back down the path toward New Hope Center. Inside she felt like she was back on the Tumbler at Misty Falls Fair—around and around her thoughts were swirling. Most of all, she wanted to tell her friends about the book that rested inside the cottonwood box that Mama had made for her. She wanted to tell Cassie and the others about her news, but there just didn't seem to be a "not-busy" time to share it! So far, today was full of early wakeup calls, flash photography, spills into the creek, and zedonks!

J.J. stopped still on the path and watched her friends who were way ahead now. There was no way she'd ever settle everyone down long enough to tell them about her news.

J.J., Navajo Princess

7

They all hurried until they came past the creek. Carefully this time, Hunter, Maddie, Iggy, Cassie, Robyn and J.J. watched their steps. By the time they arrived in the craft room, their clothes were almost dry from their surprise swim.

Trixie was assembling the children for their photograph session with Iggy. J.J. discovered that some of the children, like Maddie, didn't even appear to be sick. She couldn't help wondering what their disabilities or illnesses were that caused them to be at New Hope Center.

Other children were obviously ill. One boy was in a wheelchair. Another was breathing oxygen from a tank on wheels. A girl about Robyn's size had a brace on her neck. But all of the children had smiles on their faces. J.J. had a feeling they were smiling at Iggy. One little girl kept reaching up to touch his red hair.

"Oh, there you are. I was getting concerned," said Trixie. "Oh my goodness, Iggy, just look at you! Where have you been? In the creek?"

"Funny you should ask that," said Iggy, while J.J., Cassie, and Hunter doubled over in laughter.

"He fell into the creek, and we had to go fish him out," said Hunter.

"Had to? Or wanted to?" asked Trixie, with a knowing smile. "And Miss Maddie. Look at you...you're damp too! And you all smell like the creek. Phew!" Trixie pinched her nostrils together and made a funny face. The other children laughed and laughed.

As Iggy was taking pictures, he used all the techniques of a professional photographer to get them to do exactly what they needed to do for the camera— smile. He was a natural. J.J. noticed the room was abuzz with cheerful voices as Iggy finally placed his camera in its case.

"When can we see the photographs?" asked a pale but bright-eyed little boy in the wheelchair.

Iggy replied, "I'll ask my dad to help me develop them right away. I'll bring you a copy of the picture in a few days."

"Alright!" said the boy. "I'm Ben. Look me up when you come back to New Hope."

"I will," promised Iggy. "See ya around!"

Maddie stayed in the craft room to begin a new art project with Nurse Trixie. But J.J., Cassie, Hunter, and Iggy slipped down the hall to Robyn's room.

Robyn flipped on the light and sighed. She sank

onto the floor into a tired little heap and leaned her head against the wall. Everyone was still damp, so they joined Robyn on the yellow, orange, and lime woven throw rug.

"I hope you all enjoyed our zedonk surprise," said a very tired Robyn.

"Yes, it was so much fun!" exclaimed Cassie. "But I hope you didn't overdo it."

"I'm okay," said Robyn. "I guess I did try to do too much, but it just feels so good to walk on my own! That's all I want to do is go, go, go! Sometimes my body starts telling me to slow down again, but I don't want to!"

J.J. took a deep cleansing breath. Why did she feel so impatient? Even though she kept trying to keep it to herself, she was nearly bursting to tell them about her Navajo book. But she still couldn't seem to find the right time to tell her friends about her discoveries about herself and her family.

"There have been so many pieces of good news today," Cassie reflected.

"Yeah," said Iggy, who started counting the blessings on his fingers. "Robyn's going home and she's off crutches, and we have a new friend named Rufus!" Everyone laughed at that.

"Not bad for one day full of secrets and surprises," said Hunter. Then he looked across the circle at the others.

"And J.J. has something to tell us, I think. Don't you J.J.?"

In amazement, J.J. looked at her new friend. "What makes you say that, Hunter?"

"I don't know. You've been sort of quiet, except when you're talking to yourself," he teased. "I heard you mumbling something about your family. What is that about?"

"Well," admitted J.J., "I have been wanting to tell you all that I had a surprise from my mother when I got home from Cassie's last night."

Cassie cupped J.J.'s hand in hers. "Do you want to tell us?" she asked.

"What is it?" asked Iggy.

J.J. looked into her friends' eyes. It was obvious that J.J. had each one's attention. They were ready to listen. Her own eyes and voice grew softer, as she sighed with relief and began.

"My mom gave me something very special last night that tells me about my Navajo family heritage," she said.

"It is a keepsake book, with my mother's paintings and sketches and photographs of my family far away in Arizona. There are pictures of family members that I haven't seen since we moved to Misty Falls. There are photos of Grandmother Teresa and me when I was little. There is one photo of my grandmother selling her crafts at Canyon de Chelley. I know it would be just a silly old book to someone else, but it has shown me who I am. "

"*Nascha*, the Navajo Princess," whispered Cassie.

Hunter's eyes were wide as he asked, "Are you really a Navajo princess?"

"Not really," J.J. said, smiling. "I just pretend sometimes. I think I'd like to go home to meet members of my clan that I don't remember. I definitely want to spend time with Grandmother Teresa. Cassie's family has given me a chance to visit next summer, when they travel out west on vacation. I hope my mother will allow me to go."

Robyn's eyes lit up. "Oh, you're going out west? How wonderful! I used to live in California. It would be fun to go back and visit. I'm happy for you, J.J."

"But," began Iggy, his face turning red, "if you go, J.J., what if you decide to stay there with your family? What if you decide not to come back? Misty Falls wouldn't be the same without you. Please say you won't move back to the Navajo Reservation, away from all of us. You won't, will you? I mean, you're pretty nice for a girl. I've kind of gotten used to you."

J.J. laughed. "Thanks, Iggy! Don't worry, I'm just hoping to visit someday. My mom and I have a home here in Misty Falls now. I've been here since I was five. I don't want to move away."

"What a relief! I don't know what I'd do without my best friend. Iggy, don't ever scare me like that again!" exclaimed Cassie. Then she added timidly, "I hope your mother wasn't upset that we asked you to go with us to Arizona next summer."

J.J. hugged Cassie, who was sitting next to her. "Don't worry, Cass. Mom isn't upset. She just wants to make sure I'm safe. You see, we left the Reservation partly because my father was angry. He was not happy that Mom became a Christian. He didn't want to stay married to my mother. And he didn't want me to become a Christian. He even threatened to take me away from my mother to prevent her from telling me about Jesus."

"Why?" asked Iggy. "I thought parents want their kids to know about Jesus."

J.J. explained. "The old Navajo beliefs don't include Jesus. So Jesus is a stranger to many Navajo families. My dad wanted nothing to do with Jesus Christ. He stayed angry most of the time and got drunk a lot. That's why I lived with my grandmother in the old hogan before we moved here."

Cassie waved her hands. "Wait, wait! Why do you want to go back, if your dad is angry? Wouldn't you be scared?" asked Cassie.

J.J. shrugged. "He's my father, Cass. I would like to see him again, to see if he has changed his mind. I hope so. If not, I hope we could be friends, anyway. Jesus loves him, whether he loves Jesus or not. So I love him too. Besides, I have lots of other family members there. My cousins, aunts, uncles, and grand-mother live on the Navajo Reservation near Canyon de Chelley."

"J.J., what is a hogan?" asked Robyn.

"It's a one-room house built in a circle with a high dome-shaped roof. Grandmother Teresa's hogan is made of wood with a mud sealer to keep the wind and rain out. The fireplace is in the middle of the room. I remember standing in the doorway watching the sun come up with Grandmother. I remember holding onto her long, green skirt and how it smelled of herbs that she ground on the grinding stone outside near her garden."

"Wow," said Iggy. "It sounds like a scene out of a movie."

Cassie looked hopeful, as she asked, "Will your mother let you go with our family next year to visit the Navajo Reservation?"

"Well, she didn't say yes, but she didn't say no, either. That's good enough for me right now."

Robyn got up and went to her computer. "Let's see if there's a Native American Web site."

At the thought, J.J. exclaimed, "Oh Robyn, could we? I never even thought of that! It just occurred to me last night that maybe I could start emailing my cousins, but I have to get their email addresses first."

Robyn clicked her mouse very quickly, J.J. noted. She could surf the Web very efficiently! In a matter of minutes, Robyn had found a Web site. J.J. could feel her heart beating inside her chest. Ever since her mom had given her the wonderful keepsake book, J.J. was hungry for more information about her people and her clan.

First, Hunter read an interesting fact, as Robyn surfed around: "Awesome! There are 557 Native American tribes in 33 states...Sioux, Choctaw, Navajo, Cherokee, wow! The list goes on and on! They make up a total of about 2.4 million people!"

"That's a lot of people," remarked Iggy. "Do they all live on reservations?"

"No, this page says just 1.3 million of them live on reservations," read J.J. "Let's see. That would be a little more than half of all Native Americans living on the reservations. I guess that I'm part of the other million or so who don't live on reservations in the United States. Wow! There are lot of Native Americans like me living all over that I didn't know about."

"Oh look, here's a Web page about the Navajo Nation! And travel information. Oh Cassie, look!" J.J. read over Robyn's shoulder.

"Maybe we can get ideas of what to see on our summer vacation next year," said Cassie. "What else is there? Let's come back to this Web site later." Robyn saved the address in her favorites folder so that she could pull it up anytime J.J. wanted.

Quickly, Robyn clicked a "customs" icon on the screen. Navajo customs and cultural information was

Navajo Country

(J.J.'s grandmother and other family members live on a reservation in this region)

listed. There were even recipes that included Navajo fry bread.

"Look," said Iggy. "That picture of fry bread looks like Cassie's stinky poodles."

Everyone laughed. Cassie shook her head. "You're hopeless, Iggy Potts. For Pete's sake, they are not stinky poodles. They're Snickerdoodles," she said.

While Cassie and Iggy quibbled, J.J. got even more excited and pointed to the computer screen.

"Look everyone, there is the Navajo Nation's Seal! My mother painted that seal for the book she gave to me. It looks just like that."

"Wow," said Iggy. "It has a lot of colors. What a cool design."

"Everything on the seal has a meaning," said J.J. proudly.

"Let's see what's on this page," Robyn said. She got a funny expression on her face when she surfed the Web, with her tongue peeking out of the corner of her mouth. Suddenly, a list of names and Web addresses appeared on the screen.

"Look! Does your cousin's name happen to be Cole?" asked Robyn.

"Yes, and Tera too," said J.J. "Why?"

Robyn pointed. "Right there! There's a Cole Graystone! Could he be your cousin, J.J.?"

J.J. gasped. She couldn't take her eyes off the computer monitor. "My cousin! You found my cousin!"

J.J., Navajo Princess

8

J.J. felt dizzy with excitement. She exclaimed gratefully, "Robyn, you are so good at surfing the Net! I can't believe you've found my cousin. Go to that site, please!"

Robyn clicked the mouse again, and they saw on the screen:

Welcome to the home page of Cole and Tera Graystone.

J.J. hopped up and down. "Oh look—there they both are! My cousins!"

"Look!" said Hunter. "Man, I'm going to ask my parents to buy me a computer of my own. I can help pay for it with the money I've made mowing lawns. This Web site stuff is cool. I'll bet I could find lots of information on flying and jets."

In a moment, a color graphic of Cole and Tera appeared. They were wearing T-shirts and jeans and had suntanned skin and dark hair like J.J.'s. Even their eyes had the same shape and color as J.J.'s.

"Wow," said Iggy. "Look everybody, look!"

Cassie and J.J. hopped in place. J.J. felt like dancing! "What does it say, Robyn?" she asked. "I'm too nervous to read!"

So Robyn began to read. Here is what the home page said:

"Hi, our names are Cole and Tera Graystone. We live near Flagstaff, Arizona, with our mother and father. We live in a house on the Navajo Reservation. Every summer, we visit our grandmother who lives outside the town of Chinle (Chin-lee). We help her sell her crafts at Canyon de Chelley to the tourists who come to visit. Back at her home, we help Grandmother take care of her sheep, because she is old now. We like to spend the night with her in her traditional Navajo house, called a hogan. Her hogan has no electricity or running water, so when we stay with her, we draw water from a nearby spring. We have to play and work by the light of the fire and the sun shining through the doorway. Grandmother makes us fry bread and honey to eat, which is our favorite dish…"

Iggy patted J.J. on the back. "Robyn has found your family, J.J.!" J.J. was so happy that she squealed with delight. How she longed to be there with Cole and Tera and Grandmother right now!

Finally Hunter asked, "Go ahead, Robyn. What else do Cole and Tera say?"

Robyn continued to read their home page.

"We have a big family. There are so many in our clan that we have not met everyone who belongs to our family yet. We go to school and learn the Navajo customs and the Navajo language. We are proud to be from the Navajo Nation and speak the Navajo language that our ancestors spoke. Now we can understand some things that our Grandmother says to us in Navajo."

J.J. could barely see. The happy tears in her eyes were hard to see through. She swallowed hard and brushed away a tear that had escaped down her cheek.

"This is amazing," said Cassie, smiling at J.J.

Hunter put up his hand. "Wait, this is the best part. Listen! Go ahead, Robyn. Read that paragraph."

"This summer, we went to Vacation Bible School in our cousin's yard. We made picture frames and glued shells on the frame. We played some great games and sang songs. We heard true stories about Jesus. We found out that Jesus is God's Son, and He paid for all the bad things called sin that people do. Jesus had to die on the cross to pay for our sin. It is a free gift. So now we are Christians—followers of Jesus. We are happy and proud to belong to Jesus. Jesus

loves the Navajo people and all the other
people in the world. No matter who you are
or where you are, Jesus loves you, too."

Robyn stopped reading. She turned away from the
computer and said thoughtfully, "I remember at the
picnic, you all told me about Jesus. Now J.J.'s cousins
are telling me about Jesus through the Internet! He
must be a very special person."

"Come to church with us Sunday," said J.J., sniffing
and wiping her eyes. "We will hear more about Jesus
there."

"Okay," said Robyn. "I'll ask Aunt Felicia and Uncle
Steve to come, too."

"And Robyn," continued J.J., "thank you, thank you,
thank you! You practically brought my cousins right
into this room! I feel like I have had a visit with Cole,
Tera, and Grandmother Teresa. Could you do me
another favor?"

"Anything," Robyn said cheerfully.

"Would you print a copy of Cole and Tera's home
page and their picture graphic? I'd like to put it in my
keepsake book."

"Piece of cake," said Robyn. She clicked "print." The
page printed out just as they heard a knock at the
door.

Hunter answered the door, and there were Nurse
Trixie and J.J.'s mom. "Look who's here," said Nurse
Trixie. J.J.'s mom was still dressed up from work and

looked beautiful in her red skirt, jacket, and dangly gold earrings.

J.J. hugged her mom. "I didn't know you were picking us up."

"I got a call from Mrs. Holbrook this afternoon. I offered to come by, so that she could finish a project she was working on. It was right on my way home from work," Ms. Graystone explained.

"Did you have a good day, Mama?" J.J. asked.

"Yes, but I'm still having trouble finding an exhibit to replace the one that canceled. Everywhere I've tried, I've run into conflicts," she said with a sigh. "But what about you? Have you had a good day, kids?" asked Ms. Graystone.

"Absolutely great!" exclaimed J.J. She showed her mother the paper that Robyn had just printed out. "Look!"

As her mom read the paper, her eyes seemed to grow twice as wide. "Oh my goodness," said Ms. Graystone. "What do you know? Tera and Cole! And look, here's their email address!"

J.J. hadn't noticed that on their home page until it was printed on paper. "Now I can write Cole and Tera as much as I want," said J.J., "That is, if I may use your laptop computer."

"Of course you can," said her mother affectionately. With each passing moment, she hugged J.J. more firmly.

"Robyn found the Web site for me," explained J.J. "Wasn't that nice of her?"

"Very nice," said Ms. Graystone. "Thank you for your help, Robyn."

Just then, Robyn found another icon that looked like a little hut of some kind. She clicked on it. Suddenly there appeared a picture graphic of a real hogan.

"So this is what a hogan looks like," said Hunter. "Wow, it's really well constructed. I bet it would be fun to live in a hogan."

"If you like to work, that is," said Ms. Graystone, with a laugh. "I remember staying pretty busy when I was growing up in my mother's hogan."

J.J. looked closer at the screen. "Oh look, if we click on this icon, we can get the blueprints on how to make a replica of a real hogan."

"Wow," Iggy said. "Cassie, I bet your dad could build one of these in his woodworking shop."

"Wouldn't that be fun, if we had our own hogan to meet in?" asked Cassie. "It could be our meeting room for talks and parties." Then Cassie's hazel eyes flashed with excitement.

"Hey, I have a great idea! Dad has some extra wood lying in a corner of the barn that he isn't going to use. Maybe I could ask him to help us build a hogan!"

J.J. and her mother looked at Cassie, and then at each other. J.J. didn't know who was more excited, herself or her mom. She was pretty sure it was her mother. Before she knew it, Mama was laughing and dancing with Iggy around Robyn's room! Then she danced with Robyn and Cassie and Hunter and Maddie and a startled Nurse Trixie.

"Mama," laughed J.J., "what has gotten into you? I've never seen you like this!"

"Oh, Cassie just gave me a great idea for the children's museum exhibit, and contacts to call on!" said Ms. Graystone. "Would you all like to help me construct the next exhibit for the children's museum?"

"Huh?" asked Iggy.

"You mean a hogan?" asked J.J. in wonder.

"Yes, and all sorts of Navajo displays to go with it, showing some examples of the culture and customs of the Navajo people," said Ms. Graystone. "I have paintings, sketches, and jewelry that we could put in the exhibit, if Mr. Holbrook will help us build the hogan using the blueprints on this Web site that Robyn has found."

Robyn printed off the blueprints for the hogan. Ms. Graystone folded the piece of paper and tucked it into her purse.

"Let's go talk him into it," suggested Cassie. "I think this will be lots of fun!"

"Me too!" said J.J. "It will help me feel closer to my Grandmother Teresa, to have a real hogan right here in Misty Falls!"

Adventures in Misty Falls

"I will help you prepare the exhibit, Ms. Graystone," offered Robyn. "It'll be fun!"

"I'll help, count me in," said Hunter.

"Me too," said Iggy. "And if you need a good photographer, I'm available."

"Oh, thank you," said Ms. Graystone. "This is a huge concern that has just melted away. Now, there is so much to do, so much to plan, and not much time! We'd better go."

With that, they all bid Nurse Trixie and Robyn good-bye and headed to Cassie's house. J.J.'s head was spinning with ideas. She couldn't wait to get to the farm and ask Mr. Holbrook for his help. And she couldn't wait to email her cousins, Tera and Cole! She had the full support of her friends. Today, dreams were coming true all over the place. Now, if she could only see her grandmother...not in a photograph or over the Internet, but face to face!

J.J., Navajo Princess

9

The ride to Cassie's farm was bubbly and loud.
Everyone seemed to talk at once. Ideas seemed to
multiply as they rode along. J.J. couldn't wait to
get there. She wanted to ask Mr. Holbrook for his
help right away. Seeing her mother so happy had
boosted her spirits. She also wanted to hug Gracie
and whisper all her good news.

As the car pulled into the driveway and came to
a stop, they piled out quickly. Mr. Holbrook was
grilling hamburgers on the patio. He was flipping
them with an extra long spatula, and a backward
baseball cap was nested on his head.

The boys raced to his side. "Hi Mr. Holbrook,"
said Hunter. "What's up?"

"Good to see you again, Hunter. I believe we
met at the picnic at New Hope Center."

"Yes Sir, thanks for having me over tonight," he
said.

You're more than welcome," said Mr. Holbrook.

Iggy said, "Enough of this polite talk. Boy!
Those burgers sure smell good. Do you think

they'll take long to finish cooking? I'm starved."

Mr. Holbrook chuckled. "Not long at all, fellas. Just hold on a little longer. Hello Carol—and thank you for bringing the kids back for Meg. She has had her hands full today."

"Not a problem, Joe," said Ms. Graystone. "It has actually worked out for the best. The children have helped me come up with a great idea for an exhibit for the children's museum. I could use your advice and your help, if you are available."

"What do you need?" Cassie's father asked.

"Well," said Cassie, "for starters, we have a great use in mind for the extra wood in the old barn."

"Oh?" asked Mr. Holbrook. "I'm sure glad I didn't throw it away, then. I was just thinking about hauling it off in the morning."

J.J. breathed a sigh of relief. "I'm glad we caught you. Could we use the wood to build a hogan?"

"What's a hogan?" asked Mr. Holbrook.

His question stirred up Iggy, Hunter, Cassie, and especially J.J. They all started answering Mr. Holbrook at once, so that no one could be understood.

"Wait a minute!" Iggy said, with his hand held high over his head. "Let J.J. tell him."

J.J. looked at her mother, then she swallowed hard. This was her big chance to enlist Mr. Holbrook's help. Finally J.J. began to explain about her mother's exhibit, the need for the wood in Mr. Holbrook's barn and the need for his expert help as a woodworker to build the hogan for the museum exhibit. She asked her mother to give Mr. Holbrook the blueprints for constructing the hogan.

Mr. Holbrook took off his cap and scratched his head as he examined the plan. "Well now, I've got some cows to haul over to the next county tomorrow. After that, I'm free. We can get started about 10:00 A.M. I suspect we could build the frame here. From the blueprints, that looks like a full day's work or more. Then later this week, we could haul it to the museum and finish it up there. Would that work?"

J.J. smiled at her mother, who said, "Why, yes, it would work just fine!"

"Thank you, Mr. H. I knew you'd help us. Mama, isn't this great?" said J.J. excitedly.

"Certainly is," said Ms. Graystone. "Thank you Joe. You are very generous. I'm sure the museum appreciates your willingness to help. We'll discuss the details later."

"I feel like celebrating!" exclaimed Cassie. "Anybody feel like another swim? This time we can play "Try to Find the Bottom of Possum Creek Swimming Hole. No one has found the bottom yet, you know."

"What are we waiting for? I've already got my creek-swimming clothes on!" said Iggy, reminding them of his spill into the stream behind New Hope Center.

"Let's go!" said Hunter. "Race ya!"

Iggy, J.J. and Cassie took on Hunter's challenge. Off they ran at full speed across the south field to the swimming hole. In one area of the creek was a deep, unexplainable hole, where the waters were colder and deeper than anywhere else in the creek. There was a rock that was perfect for diving off into the water.

They took turns jumping and diving into the refreshing waters for the next half-hour. Suddenly, Iggy started complaining. "I'm starved. Do you think it's time to eat yet?"

Cassie teased him. "The next game we will play is called 'Try to Find the Bottom of Iggy's Bottomless Pit'—his stomach!" Everyone laughed.

"Well, aren't you guys hungry too?" Iggy asked.

Hunter looked at Iggy, then J.J., then Cassie. "Let's eat." The girls agreed.

Back across the field they ran, dripping all the way. For the second time that day, they dripped dry. Mr. Holbrook had built a fire, which served as an additional dryer for the wet clothing they wore. The hamburgers tasted extra good, because they were so hungry.

Later, the girls went to check on Gracie and Chester. The horses were both standing at the gate, waiting to be led back from the pasture to the barn for their scoop of grain and water. Meanwhile, the boys and Mr. Holbrook began to take inventory of the wood supply for the hogan. Ms. Graystone and Mrs. Holbrook chatted beside the fire in their lawn chairs.

As the girls saw to their horses' needs, they finally were able to share a private moment.

"Cassie," said J.J., "I'm so excited about finding the Web site today. Wasn't it great of Robyn to find it?"

"It sure was. I love Robyn. I'm so happy that she will be going home this weekend. It seems good things are happening all around," Cassie answered.

"Yes," J.J. had that faraway look. "If only Grandmother Teresa could know that I love her. All of this talk about hogans has me really missing her. I think I'll write her tonight, and write my cousins an email message."

Later that evening, after her shower, J.J. did just that. She wrote:

> *Dear Grandmother Teresa, I miss you. I have told my friends in Misty Falls about you and the hogan where you live. We are going to build a hogan for the museum. I wish I could find a way to come and see you—maybe next summer with my friend, Cassie.*
>
> *Your "little owl,"*
> *Nascha (J.J.)*

Then she borrowed Mama's laptop and wrote an email message:

Dear Cole and Tera,

Today on the Internet, my friend Robyn found your Web page! I am so happy to read about your life on the reservation in Arizona. It sounds great! I am a Christian too! We have a lot in common. I am very proud to have a Navajo heritage. I have a cat named Frisco, and Gracie is my horse. I hope to see you next summer. If I'm allowed, I will come to the reservation to visit you and our grandmother. My friends and I are going to build a hogan for the children's museum here in Georgia. How is Grandmother Teresa? Please write me soon.

Love,

J.J. Graystone (your cousin)

Falling asleep that night was easy. J.J. was a tired princess.

J.J., Navajo Princess

10

The next day, J.J. was at Cassie's by 10:30 A.M. Already the hogan was taking shape. Mr. Holbrook, Cassie's brother Jeff, Iggy, Hunter, and Cassie were setting up a small replica of the hogan on a large sheet of plywood beside the old barn. It had six sides like her grandmother's hogan. But instead of using heavy logs to build the sides, the model hogan was being constructed with 2 x 4 strips of Mr. Holbrook's leftover lumber and sheets of plywood.

"Real hogans are much heavier and larger than our model," explained Mr. Holbrook, wiping his brow. "But I believe this will be an easier size to transport to the children's museum. We have plenty of wood, and then we will finish the out-side with a cement-mud mixture to make it look like a picture of your grandmother's hogan."

"What about a fireplace?" asked J.J. "A fireplace goes in the middle."

"Our pretend hogan will have a pretend fireplace," said Mr. Holbrook. "The children who come to the museum will have a pretty good idea about what a real hogan is like."

"Okay," said J.J. She rolled up her sleeves and helped Cassie haul wood from the barn to the building site.

By mid-afternoon, the hogan was really taking shape. Mr. Holbrook and Jeff kept working on the roof, but they let the others have the rest of the day off.

"The roof on a real hogan is very complicated, but I will try to make it look like your grandmother's roof, J.J." said Mr. Holbrook. "Then we will put on the final touches at the museum."

"I know you are doing your best," said J.J. with a friendly smile. "If it weren't for you, my mother wouldn't have an exhibit for the children's museum. And Misty Falls wouldn't have its very own hogan!"

Mr. Holbrook laughed and got back to work.

In the meantime, J.J., Cassie, and their mothers drove to the Graystone's apartment. They spent the after-noon selecting sketches, paintings, and Navajo relics from Ms. Graystone's keepsake collection. Now was the perfect time to show Cassie her special book that Mama had given her.

The girls went to the cottonwood box where J.J.'s book was stored. Cassie's eyes were bright as she waited for J.J. to lift the heavy book out of the storage box.

Just as Mama had placed the book in J.J.'s lap, now Cassie got a lap full of book.

"Oh my goodness," exclaimed Cassie, "it is heavy, just like you said!"

Cassie ran her fingers along the book's binding and opened it to the first page. There was J.J.'s baby picture and the inscription:

Jennifer Joy Graystone
Traditional Navajo Name: Nascha ("owl")
Born to Tahoma and Carol Kai Graystone
Flagstaff, Arizona

"I like your father's name—Tahoma," said Cassie.

"Me too," said J.J. "Doesn't it sound so very Navajo?"

"Yes, it does," said Cassie. She turned the pages carefully, and J.J. explained everything she knew about the photographs and sketches.

"Mama painted this one," said J.J., pointing to the landscape sketch of Canyon de Chelley. "See, down there in the canyon is where Grandmother used to take her sheep to graze in the green grass. And here is the great Seal of the Navajo Nation that we saw on the Internet."

"Did you paint this one of Frisco?" asked Cassie, pointing to a four-legged animal.

J.J. burst into laughter. "Oh Cass, that's Gracie when she was a yearling. I wasn't a very good artist, was I?"

Cassie's favorite pictures were of J.J. as a young child on the reservation. "You were so cute with your long dark hair and your chubby cheeks," she said with a giggle. "Is this your grandmother?"

"Yes," said J.J. softly. "Isn't she elegant in her turquoise earrings that she made? We were selling jewelry in the canyon to tourists."

Finally, Cassie closed the book and sighed. "J.J., you really are a Navajo Princess. Thank you for sharing your keepsake book with me. I feel like I know you even better now. I'm glad you are my friend."

J.J. patted Cassie's arm. "That feeling goes both ways. Girlfriends are forever!"

After storing the book in J.J.'s cottonwood trunk, the girls helped their mothers carry boxes to the car. The boxes were filled with paintings, sketches, and Navajo crafts. There was also a wool blanket woven by Grandmother Teresa, and a woolen wall hanging in brilliant colors. Ms. Graystone also packed turquoise jewelry and a dream-catcher that usually hung in J.J.'s window.

Finally, the car was loaded, and it was time to take the materials to the children's museum in metropolitan Atlanta.

There was barely enough room for the girls to squeeze in among the boxes in the back seat. But J.J.

J.J., Navajo Princess

and Cassie managed, while Ms. Graystone and Mrs. Holbrook rode up front.

"The museum director just loved our idea for the exhibit," J.J.'s mom was saying. "In fact, the whole staff can't wait to see our Navajo collection. I just can't thank you enough for your family's help, Meg."

"It's our pleasure. Besides, we are big fans of museums for children," said Mrs. Holbrook. "Remember, Cassie? We started visiting this museum when you were just a little girl. And only the good Lord knows how many school field trips I have chaperoned over the years to the museum, the zoo, and yes, even Braves baseball games!"

"I remember most of my school field trips to the museum," said Cassie. "It's a really neat place to visit. Maybe my favorite field trip of all time was going to the museum when the dinosaur exhibit came to Atlanta. I never get tired of exploring the exhibits."

"Me either," said J.J. "If my career as a professional horsewoman doesn't work out, I might follow in my mother's footsteps and work at the children's museum. It's fun watching the children's faces when they discover something new and exciting!"

For the rest of the afternoon, Cassie and J.J. unloaded the car, then the boxes. J.J. discovered a box of her toys from the Navajo Reservation. There were J.J.'s bangles and beads for her hair and wrists, a doll dressed in leather and beads, and a storybook about

Navajo myths. The girls made colorful southwestern information signs explaining about the hogan. They made nameplates for all of the relics, sketches, and crafts they had brought.

The room where they unloaded was completely empty when they arrived at the museum. But by the end of the day, the walls and tables were filled with sketches, paintings, wallhangings, and pottery. There was a big empty spot in the center of the room where the hogan would go. J.J. had worked so hard that her hair was falling out of its braid. She and Cassie stood back, admiring their work.

"I wonder how the boys and my dad are doing with the hogan?" said Cassie.

"Funny you should ask that," said a voice that J.J. and Cassie knew all too well.

"Iggy!" they sang in chorus.

"And Hunter!" added Cassie. "Are you finished?"

The boys pretended to stagger in and faint onto the exhibit hall floor. The girls laughed, as the boys got up. Indeed, they were dirty, sweaty boys from their hard work.

But they had big smiles across their faces. Behind them, Mr. Holbrook and Jeff entered from the loading dock.

"Where do you want the hogan?" asked Mr. Holbrook.

J.J. gasped. "Do you mean it's here? It's ready?"

"It's here, but not finished," explained Mr. Holbrook. "We will put a mud-colored stucco finish on the outside of the hogan. But it is loaded on the truck at the loading dock."

Ms. Graystone called the museum staff helpers to support the hogan as it was carried. It took everyone, men, women, boys, and girls, lifting it together to carry it into the museum. They placed it in the very center of the room. It was grand. All J.J. had to do was pretend, and she was suddenly standing in front of her grandmother's house.

Just like Grandmother Teresa's hogan, the model had six sides, a doorway that faced the east for the morning sun, and a small window. Ms. Graystone was very excited. "We'll put the finishing touches on the inside, hang a curtain in the window and some southwestern pictures on the wall, stack some woolen blankets, add a chair, and it will look like the inside of a real hogan."

"Yes, I have a stack of firewood for the fake fireplace," said Mr. Holbrook. "We can bring that when we come back to do the stucco work."

J.J. and Cassie stood back and marveled at their work. "I can't believe how fast this has all come together," said J.J.

"Me either," said Cassie. She looked at J.J. and smiled. "Welcome to Grandmother Teresa's house!"

11

The next day, J.J. awoke with a yawn and immediately went to see if she had any email messages on Mama's laptop computer. She had two!

The first one was from Cole Graystone, her cousin. He wrote,

> *Dear J.J., thank you for writing to us! I am glad to hear from you. I do not usually get email all the way from Georgia. How are you? We hope you can come to visit next summer too. Write again soon.*
>
> *Your cousin, Cole.*

The second email message was from Tera, his sister. She wrote,

> *Hi J.J.! I am glad you wrote to Cole and me. We are going to Grandmother's today to take her into the city. She is closing down the hogan. (I am not supposed to tell you why.) Gotta go! I'll write more later.*
>
> *Your cousin, Tera*

Not supposed to tell you why? J.J. wondered what that meant. Could it be that Grandmother Teresa was sick? She never left the hogan for more than a day to sell her jewelry in the canyon. Why would she be closing up her hogan, unless she was too sick to live there anymore?

J.J. ran to her mother's room. "Mama? Where are you? Something is wrong with Grandmother Teresa!"

There was no answer. Only Frisco's purring broke the silence. J.J. ran to the window. Mama's car was already gone. *She must have left early for work today,* J.J. thought to herself.

She went to the kitchen for some juice, and there was a note from her mother on the counter:

J.J. I'll be home at noon today. Please clean your room while I'm gone. Love, Mama.

J.J. sighed. How she hated to clean her room! Besides, her muscles still ached from all the work she had done getting the exhibit ready for the children's museum. And how could she clean her room when she was so worried about Grandmother?

Picking up the phone, she called her mother's office number. No one answered. So J.J. left a voice mail message. "This is J.J., Mama. Please call me. I think something is wrong with Grandmother Teresa."

J.J. hung up the phone and sighed. She looked around at the empty house. There was nothing left to do but wait. And clean her room.

J.J., Navajo Princess

Every few minutes, J.J. ran to the window to see if Mama was back yet. The more she thought about Grandmother Teresa, the more worried she became. J.J. tried to stay busy. She made her bed and dusted her bedside table and the small dresser that used to belong to her mother when she was a girl. She picked up the clothes that were lying on the chair and the floor, and put her sandals in the closet. Her room was clean.

The phone rang. On the very first ring, J.J. ran into the hall to answer. It just had to be Mama! "Hello?"

"Hi, J.J. Whatcha doing?" It was Cassie. "Want to go to the museum with us? We're putting the stucco finish on the outside of the hogan."

"I don't think I'd better, Cass. Something is wrong with Grandmother. I don't know what yet. I'm trying to find my mother to tell her. She wasn't at the museum."

"Wait, slow down, J.J. Why do you think something is wrong with your grandmother?"

"Oh. I got an email from Cole and another one from Tera, my cousins. Tera's said something strange. It said they were taking Grandmother to the city, and they were closing down the hogan."

Cassie gasped. "Oh no, J.J.! Why would she close the hogan?"

"I don't know," agreed J.J., "Grandmother has always lived at the hogan. She only leaves the house to go into the canyon for the day to sell jewelry and crafts."

"You'd better stay by the phone," said Cassie. "If we see your mother at the museum we will ask her to call you."

"That makes me feel better," said J.J. "Thank you. Oh Cassie, say a prayer for Grandmother Teresa."

"I will," said Cassie.

J.J. hung up the phone and went to the big cottonwood storage box. Once more, she pulled out the big keepsake book. She flipped over to the photographs of Grandmother. Big tears filled J.J.'s eyes, as she wondered, *Will I ever see my grandmother again?"*

Frisco seemed to know that J.J.'s heart was troubled. He curled up next to her on the floor beside the cottonwood trunk of keepsakes.

Suddenly, something bumped the front door. Then there was a key in the lock. J.J.'s heart jumped into her throat, as she hopped up still holding her keepsake book.

As she walked toward the front door, it opened. There was her mother. "Oh Mama," said J.J., bursting into tears. "Something is wrong with Grandmother. You'd better call Aunt Joan!"

"Why?" Ms. Graystone said as she put her arms around J.J.

"Tera wrote me and said they were taking Grandmother away to the city and closing down the hogan," J.J. sobbed.

"I know," said Mama.

J.J. stopped crying and looked up into her mother's face. "What? You know?"

"Yes, you see," said Mama, turning to the open door, "someone has come a very long way to see you."

J.J. looked at the doorway. In a moment, there appeared an elderly woman in a long tiered skirt with sunbaked skin and mysterious indigo eyes. "Grandmother? Oh Grandmother, you've come to Misty Falls!"

"*Nascha*," said Grandmother Teresa. Her arms opened wide. J.J. let the book drop to the floor, and J.J. ran into her grandmother's loving embrace. It was one of the most joyful moments of J.J.'s life.

It took a long time for J.J. to calm down, but she finally did. And she learned that Grandmother Teresa had come to Atlanta to help with the children's museum exhibit.

Mama explained that she had met Grandmother at the airport that morning. "The museum paid for Grandmother's trip," Mama said. "She is going to receive the school groups into the hogan and demonstrate her crafts."

"Why didn't you tell me she was coming?" asked J.J., who was all smiles.

Mama winked. "That would have spoiled the surprise," she said slyly.

"How long can she stay with us?" asked J.J.

"As long as she wants," said Mama.

Adventures in Misty Falls

"It was a one-way ticket to Atlanta."

That night, Grandmother Teresa shared J.J.'s bedroom. She sang old Navajo songs in the moonlight that danced on the curtains. Just like when J.J. was very small, she fell asleep to Grandmother's lullabies.

When J.J. next saw the hogan at the children's museum, it was finished. The stucco finish on the outside made it look more real. Grandmother smiled from ear to ear when she saw the hogan and laughed with pleasure.

Mama translated Grandmother's words for J.J. "She says this hogan is cleaner than her hogan on the reservation, and that it is a good trade."

J.J. laughed at her grandmother's joke. Later the same day, J.J. introduced all of her friends to Grandmother Teresa at Cassie's farm. Grandmother liked Iggy's red hair and Hunter's polite manners. She hugged Cassie like she was another granddaughter.

Grandmother Teresa said something in Navajo. The tones and rhythm of her words were beautiful, even though J.J. couldn't understand them.

Ms. Graystone translated. "Grandmother wants to see you ride your horse, J.J. You too, Cassie."

On the way to the barn, Cassie exclaimed, "Now I know why you love your grandmother so much! She is very nice and grandmotherly. I already love her."

"I can't argue with that!" said J.J.

Quickly, the girls brushed out their horses' coats. J.J.

bridled Gracie and waited for Cassie to finish getting Chester ready for a ride. Soon, they walked their horses out of the barn and mounted at the practice ring.

J.J. clucked to Gracie, who obeyed in an instant. It took a little longer for Cassie to coax Chester into obeying. But finally, the girls were both on their way. Grandmother walked to the practice ring to watch with Mrs. Holbrook and Ms. Graystone.

Faster and faster, J.J. and Gracie circled the ring until they were at a full canter. She slowed to a stop at Grandmother's side. Grandmother stroked Gracie's neck, then J.J.'s smiling indigo eyes met her grandmother's. J.J. remembered the words from the Bible that Cassie had talked about. They rang in her ears once again…"Everything works together for good for those who love the Lord."

J.J. was missing her grandmother so deeply that she wanted to go to the Navajo Reservation. Instead, God had brought the Navajo Reservation to J.J.

Nascha, the Navajo Princess was truly free at last.

ROBYN FLIES HOME

"For such a long time she had waited....And it had taken forever."

Robyn's adventures continue as she finally leaves the rehabilitation center and starts the life of a normal kid. As hard as it is to leave all her friends at the center, Robyn starts school—for the first time—in the fifth grade. **But why are all the kids ignoring her? And why does that mean boy keep calling her a "crip"?**

As hard as her new life seems, Robyn's ready for the challenge. As Iggy said, "She's stronger than she looks." Everybody is about to find out that fragile Robyn is tougher than she seems.

Look for this next exciting adventure in the Misty Falls series at your local Christian bookstore.

Adventures in Misty Falls series
Robyn Flies Home
N007106
$4.99 • 1-56309-764-8 • paper

Robyn Flies Home
1-56309-764-8
N007106
$4.99

Robyn Flies Home

Renée Kent

Condensed excerpt from *Robyn Flies Home*

The funny thing about sleeping is that once a girl has slept all she needs to, she is wide awake. Robyn awoke with a start at 4:15 A.M. She couldn't stop wiggling, tossing, and turning. Finally she sat up in bed. "Well, I might as well get ready for school!"

The house was dark and still. Quietly, she tiptoed to the bathroom. Aunt Felicia had left her a basket full of bath supplies, including a loofah sponge and some skin softening bath gel that smelled like bubble gum. After a good scrubbing, Robyn was really wide awake and squeaky clean.

She had a hard time choosing which new clothes to wear to school that first day. She decided on shorts and the new top that matched her blue eyes, since that was the feature Robyn most liked about herself.

Then she made sure that everything was packed in her new book bag and set it by the front door. The first light of dawn appeared through the kitchen window as Robyn poured herself a bowl of cereal with milk.

Finally, Aunt Felicia called, "Robyn, time for school! The bus will be here in five minutes. Hurry!"

"Don't you look great in those new clothes! Here's your lunch money. Have a happy first day of school, sweetie," Aunt Felicia said.

Robyn got to the curb just in time to meet the school bus. As she climbed aboard, she smiled at the driver. The driver smiled and looked at his list of passengers.

Robyn sat down in the first seat and waved to Aunt Felicia. She was the first passenger on the bus. Butterflies were dancing inside her tummy.

At the next stop, a much older boy got on the bus. Robyn smiled, but he didn't even look as he walked past. Robyn was a little relieved that he didn't pay her any attention. He was awfully big and seemed a little scary. Farther down Eagle Bend and around the corner, the bus driver picked up two girls who looked like they were Robyn's age.

Goodie! thought Robyn. She decided to invite the

girls to sit with her. But when she opened her mouth to speak to them, the girls just giggled to each other and walked past. The more children who boarded the bus, the more frustrated Robyn grew. It didn't seem that anyone noticed her. Maybe she was invisible.

Robyn Flies Home

Finally, Robyn decided it was because she was new. "I'm going to have to try harder to make the first move," said Robyn to herself.

As the bus pulled into the school parking lot, Robyn turned around to speak to the girls sitting behind her. "Um, excuse me. Hi," she said in her most cheerful voice, "I'm Robyn. What are your names?"

The older of the girls looked at Robyn and sniffed. "Ellen," she said, looking out the window.

"I'm Elizabeth," said the other girl with the blonde ponytail. A halo of wispy natural curls framed her face. Her smile revealed braces with pink bands across her teeth. Robyn liked her instantly. Elizabeth continued, saying, "But why don't you call me Liz for short. What grade are you in?"

"Fifth," said Robyn.

"Me, too," said Liz. "Maybe we'll be in some classes together. Where did you go to school last year?"

"I've been at New Hope Center, where I had a private tutor, Mrs. Roker," said Robyn. "Have you ever heard of New Hope Center?"

Liz shook her head. "No. Is that a school?"

"No," said Robyn. "It's a place for kids who have serious health problems to get well."

"What's wrong with you?" asked Liz. "You look perfectly fine to me."

"Oh, I am fine now," said Robyn. "But I was in a car accident a long time ago and it took several years to recover."

"That must have been hard," said Liz, whose concern showed in her fair-skinned face and greenish-blue eyes.

As they waited their turn to hop off the bus, Robyn admired Liz's nail polish with different designs on each fingernail. It was finally their turn to depart. Robyn noticed that Ellen wasn't getting off the bus with them. "Aren't you going to school, Ellen?"

"I go to middle school," said Ellen, turning up her nose and looking out the window.

"Oh," said Robyn, "well, I hope you have a good day. It was nice to meet you. Bye!"

Liz and Robyn walked together into Misty Falls Elementary School. The gym was packed with students from kindergarten through fifth grade. A sea of voices filled the air with cheerful sounds. Robyn and Liz walked to the section of bleachers that was marked with a big sign that read "Fifth-graders Here."

Liz looked at Robyn, concerned. "Maybe you didn't stay at New Hope Center long enough. You're limping and your leg is still hurt," she said, pointing to some faded scars on Robyn's legs.

Robyn had forgotten that she still had a limp and scars from her injuries and surgeries. "No, I'm feeling just fine, thanks!"

"Well, if you're sure you're okay," said Liz. "Let's sit here." Robyn took the book bag off her shoulders and sat down.

"Hey," said a boy behind her, "Look at the crip!"

Robyn looked at the boy. "What did you say?"

The boy's expression was mean. "I said, you're a crip...you know, a cripple. What's the matter, are you stupid, too?"

A flood of pain washed over Robyn. Everyone sitting nearby thought it was funny, except Liz.

"Be quiet, Jason, or I'll tell the teacher what you said," Liz warned.

"Shut up, Lizard," teased the boy. "Braces Mouth!"

Liz paid no heed to him. She turned to Robyn and patted her arm. "Don't pay any attention to Jason. He's kind of a bully. Just ignore him."

The rest of the school day was a blur for Robyn. No one except Liz acted very friendly. All around Robyn, the other students seemed to stare at her, whisper, or giggle with each other.

Robyn refused to cry or run, but she wanted to do both.

In the lunchroom, another boy had walked behind her, imitating Robyn's limp. By the time she realized what he was doing, everyone in the lunchroom was looking on. They were giggling and whispering to each other about her!

I can't help it, Robyn had wanted to scream, but she said nothing. Everywhere she went, even outside at recess, she tried hard to walk like everyone else. Her right leg ached.

By the end of the school day, Robyn wasn't so sure it would be a wonderful year. What's more, Mrs. Russell had given the class a homework assignment called "What I Did This Summer". Everyone had to stand in front of the class and read theirs. Robyn heard other children talking about what they were going to report on—vacations, visiting relatives, and going to basketball camp. All Robyn had been doing was trying to walk without crutches.

When Robyn got off the bus that day, she hurried as fast as she could to get inside the house. She didn't even look back to wave good-bye to the bus driver. She knew what she had to do....

Address: http://www.mistyfallsfriends.com

Back | Forward | Stop | Refresh | Home | Search | Mail | Favorites

A WHOLE NEW MISTY FALLS WORLD IS READY FOR YOU TO EXPLORE ON THE WEB!

What do Cassie and the gang
do in their spare time?

What games do they like to play?

What does Misty Falls look like?

**Visit
www.mistyfallsfriends.com
to find out!**

DON'T MISS ANY OF THE ADVENTURES OF CASSIE AND THE MISTY FALLS GANG.

READ ALL THE BOOKS!

☐ **Cassie, You're a Winner!**
1-56309-735-4
N007116
$4.99 retail price
$1.99 through 12/31/00

☐ **Best Friends Forever?**
1-56309-734-6
N007117
$4.99

☐ **J.J., Navajo Princess**
1-56309-763-X
N007105
$4.99

☐ **Robyn Flies Home**
1-56309-764-8
N007106
$4.99

Look for books 5 and 6—available in October 2000!